TERRI DEPUE

BLOOMS

A Magnolia Creek Novel

TATE PUBLISHING
AND ENTERPRISES, LLC

Published by Tate Publishing & Enterprises, LLC
127 E. Trade Center Terrace | Mustang, Oklahoma 73064 USA
1.888.361.9473 | www.tatepublishing.com

Tate Publishing is committed to excellence in the publishing industry. The company reflects the philosophy established by the founders, based on Psalm 68:11,
"The Lord gave the word and great was the company of those who published it."

Book design copyright © 2014 by Tate Publishing, LLC. All rights reserved.
Cover design by Rodrigo Adolfo
Interior design by Gram Telen

Published in the United States of America

ISBN: 978-1-62994-415-9
Fiction / General
14.02.06

CHAPTER 1

"I only saw him for a second," Annie explained to the Seattle police officer sitting across the desk from her. "He shoved me to the ground as soon as I opened my back door."

Annie reflexively reached over to rub her shoulder where she was sure a large bruise was forming from her impact with the pavement. With her other hand she tucked her straight, dark blonde hair behind her ears and winced at the pain that slight movement caused her. "He must have heard my car but didn't have time to get out before I got to the back door. I only caught a glimpse of a gray hoodie and dark jeans as he jumped the fence and disappeared into the alley. It all happened so fast", she said softly, her voice trailing off as she relived the incident that took place less than an hour ago.

Shortly before that was when she learned she no longer had a job. She remembered thinking at the time that her day couldn't get any worse. *Boy,* she thought to herself, *had I ever been wrong about that.*

"Have you noticed anyone hanging around your house lately," he asked, "anyone that seemed out of place, or anyone you kept seeing over and over again?"

"No," Annie replied, "I don't remember anyone like that, but I usually come and go through the back door."

"Where do you work?" the officer asked her, typing skillfully on his keyboard with his two index fingers. "Is it normal for you to be gone during the middle of the day?"

"Well," Annie answered slowly, "I used to work as a substitute teacher so yes, I was usually gone during the day."

"Used to?" the officer asked, looking up from his keyboard. "How long have you been unemployed?"

Annie glanced unnecessarily at her watch and replied, "About two hours."

The police officer sat back and scratched his head, looking at Annie so intently she thought she might no longer be able to hold back her tears. "Can I give you some advice Miss Reed?" the officer said after a long moment. When Annie nodded, afraid to speak for fear of crying, he said, "I have a daughter about your age and I'm going to tell you what I would tell her."

"Okay." Annie swallowed and braced herself, not sure of what was coming next. Based on her day so far, she was not getting her hopes up.

"Move," he said pragmatically. "This neighborhood is no place for a young woman living alone." He continued looking at her intently, all thoughts of the incident report momentarily forgotten. "Do you know that your case is my third one today where a young woman has been robbed or had her home burglarized? The third one today," he repeated calmly. "And I haven't even had lunch." The officer leaned back in his chair and looked squarely at Annie, clearly finished with what he had to say. He fully expected her to cry. Instead, she began to smile.

"Thank you" she said earnestly. "I'm actually going to take your advice. As soon as we're done here, I'm going home to pack."

Annie stood in the kitchen of her small apartment, looking out the window at the overcast skies that were characteristic of winter in the Pacific Northwest. As she reflected on the events of the day, she was convinced that moving to Magnolia Creek was the right thing to do. She had assured the police officer that she was serious about heeding his advice and that she would begin packing today.

As Annie took stock of her possessions, she decided that she needed a plan. Item one on her list: call Mom and Dad. If she was going to go through with this, and she was, she would need their help. As she sat at the kitchen table to write her to-do list, Annie's mind wandered back to the day nearly a month ago when her mother called to tell her Grandma Abby passed away.

Annie had cried softly as she listened to her mother talk about her Grandma Abby in the past tense. She loved her grandmother and treasured her childhood memories of the time they spent together. As Annie's mother relayed the details of her own mother's passing, Annie's mind took her back to the day she and her parents left Magnolia Creek, the small town in southeastern Virginia where she had been born.

Annie stood by the mailbox at the edge of the driveway, waiting anxiously for her grandfather's old truck to come around the corner. Grandma Abby had promised that she would have a going away present for her granddaughter to take with her, something special to remember her by. The necklace her grandmother had given her that day had a gold daisy-shaped pendant with *You Are My Sunshine* engraved on the back. When her mother had first told her the sad news, Annie had instinctively reached for the pendant she still wore. It connected her to her grandmother in a very special way.

Soon she would be connected in a more tangible way. Annie was going to live in her grandmother's house. Or rather, *her* house as Grandma Abby had left her house, property, and all of her belongings to Annie.

When Annie opened her eyes and looked at the clock, she was surprised to see it was already eight thirty. There was light streaming in through her window and she could smell coffee wafting in from the kitchen. Annie turned to put her feet on the floor and then sank back onto the bed as the events of the previous day played through her mind.

Still lost in thought, Annie walked softly into the kitchen wearing her pajamas and a pair of thick cotton socks. She slowly poured herself a cup of coffee and took a seat at the kitchen table across from her mother who was already on her second cup.

Mary watched her daughter closely, curious how she was feeling this morning. Annie had made a big decision yesterday and when they spoke last night Annie had asked them to come over to talk about it. She and Pete had arrived early and let themselves in.

"Where's Dad?" Annie asked her mother.

"Oh, you know him," Mary replied casually, "he needs to have something to do so he decided he'd better have a look at that old car of yours before you try to drive it across the country."

Annie gazed absently at her mother and sipped her coffee, lost in her own thoughts.

"Annie," her mother said gently, "did you sleep?"

"Off and on" Annie replied, "but I actually feel rested."

Her mother smiled and said, "It's because you made your decision, honey. This was a big one and I suspect it was weighing heavily on your mind. How do you feel about it now? Any concerns?"

"Honestly, no" Annie replied. "I still can't get over how calm I am about the whole thing. It just feels right. I think the first thing is for me to figure out what to take and how to get there."

"Well don't worry about the trip," Marie assured her. "Your dad will take care of that for you. What you need to focus on is what you want to take and how soon you want to leave."

Annie and her mother were busy making lists when her dad walked in through the back door, wiping his hands on a greasy rag. "Morning, honey," he said to Annie as he leaned down to give her a kiss on the cheek. "Morning," Annie replied brightly. "So what's the verdict? Will my car make the trip?"

"Let's just say we should explore other options," her dad said with a grin.

The good news was that for the first time in her adult life, Annie could afford to look at other options. Along with the house and property there was a small inheritance. If Annie lived frugally, she could pay off her student loans and still have enough money to live on for several months. The house was paid for and according to the accountant there was an escrow fund to cover the taxes. For the moment, she was set. All she needed to do now was pick up her life, leave behind her family and friends, and move to a small southeastern Virginia town she had not set foot in since she was eight years old.

Let the adventure begin! she thought with a hint of excitement.

CHAPTER 2

Annie woke to the morning sun streaming through her bedroom window. After unpacking her suitcase and putting fresh linens on the bed, Annie had crawled under the covers and slept soundly through the night. She had arrived at her new home late in the afternoon and found the key under the flowerpot on the back porch, exactly where Grandma Abby's accountant Mr. Duffy had said it would be. He was the executor of Abby's will and was Annie's only contact in town.

It had been almost two months since anyone had lived in the house and it needed a good airing out. As Annie lay in bed contemplating her day, she made a mental to-do list. First on her agenda was a good look around the property. It had been twenty years since Annie had last seen this place and she was curious to see how much she remembered from those days.

Fishing a granola bar out of her bag, Annie grabbed her jacket and headed out the back door. The orchard beckoned. It was early spring and several of the fruit trees were just starting to blossom. The air was cold but the sun was up and it promised to be a beautiful day. Having lived most of her life in the Seattle area, Annie was just happy it wasn't raining.

She stepped off the back porch and headed toward the barn. Her Grandpa Ben had passed away when Annie was very young, but the few memories she had of him were vivid and comforting. As she neared the barn, she thought of him tinkering on one thing or another inside the barn with the doors flung open wide, whistling while he worked. He seemed happy out there among his tractors and mowers and odds and ends. Annie remembered his smile, as he would roll out from under the truck with dirt and grease smeared on his hands and face to talk with her when she came to see him.

Annie was tempted to open the barn doors and take a quick peek inside but decided that could wait for another time when she could explore it fully. She could still make out some of the old red paint that was the barn's original color. *Now it looks more like weathered wood*, she thought, *but it appears to be sturdy and there are no signs of disrepair.* She made a mental note to add exploring the barn to her to-do list.

Annie continued down the slightly overgrown path from the far side of the barn that led into the orchard beyond. Annie loved the woods, and memories of walks with her Grandpa Ben surfaced as she grew closer.

Annie stepped under the canopy of trees and felt that she had been transported to another time. As she continued walking into the orchard, all sense of time and place vanished and she felt at peace. She didn't know how else to explain it, but it felt like heaven. There was no cold wind among the trees and the birds that were chirping loudly and swooping around just outside the orchard were noticeably quiet. Annie felt peaceful here, as if it were a place of tranquility and rest.

Continuing slowly down the path, she noticed a wooden bench set back from the path in a small clearing. As she walked toward the bench, Annie noticed a roughly hewn wooden cross that appeared to be set into the ground on a small mound of earth, the wooden bench near its base. Annie was mesmerized by the vision of what appeared to be a prayer garden in the middle of the orchard. It must have been added after she moved away because she certainly would have remembered it.

Annie approached the bench to rest for a moment and say a prayer for her grandparents. As she sat down on the bench facing the cross, Annie was overcome by a sense of home. She realized with certainty that her Grandma Abby had placed this bench here so she could come and talk to Grandpa Ben after he passed away.

For Annie, it would become a place to think, pray, and reflect on life. As she sat there on that first day, she let go of her worries and doubts about what was to come and surrendered to the moment. When she rose a few moments later, she noticed the birds chirping in the trees above her and the wind rusting the leaves at her feet. She smiled as she stood to walk back to the house and into her new life.

....

CHAPTER 3

When Annie returned to the house, she hung her jacket on a hook in the mudroom and pulled off her boots. She started in the kitchen and went around to every room downstairs and opened the windows to let in the fresh air. By this time the sun was high in the sky and the breeze was mild and balmy. Grandma Abby had sheer curtains on all of the windows and Annie loved to see them flutter softly in the breeze. It reminded her of warm summer nights lying in bed listening to the grownups talking and laughing in the backyard.

While she was upstairs opening the bedroom windows, Annie thought she heard a car pull into the driveway. *Who on earth could that be?* she wondered. *A neighbor perhaps?* She was just heading down the stairs when she heard the knock.

Annie opened the door to three women who looked to be well into their eighties. She did not recognize them, but thought it was likely they were friends of her late grandmother. The leader of the trio was a short,

....

16

stout woman with white hair that fell in soft, unkempt curls around her face. She smiled at Annie with a wide grin, her bright blue eyes dancing.

"Good morning, Annie!" she announced cheerfully from the other side of the screened door. "You probably don't remember us, but we're friends of your grandmother's. I'm Winnie, this is Betty Lou, and that's Lillian. We wanted to stop by to welcome you home and to tell you how happy we are that you are here."

The two women behind Winnie were both slightly taller and thinner than their friend, but with the same white hair and warm smiles.

"Please come in," Annie offered, standing back to let them pass. As she closed the door behind them, she noticed the old yellow car parked in the driveway. It was one of the biggest cars she had ever seen, and probably the shiniest. The chrome mirrors, bumpers, and trim appeared new but she doubted that was the case. More likely this old car had spent most of its fifty or sixty years in someone's garage, driven only to church. The thought of Winnie being that proverbial "little old lady" made her laugh.

"It's good to see the shades up and the windows open," Winnie was saying as Annie's attention returned to the women now standing in the middle of her grandmother's living room. *My living room,* she corrected herself silently. *It was now my living room.*

"Lillian here brought you some homemade cinnamon buns that will melt in your mouth," Winnie said excitedly. "Everyone around here knows she makes the best buns, isn't that right, Lillian?" she asked expectantly.

Lillian nodded and agreed modestly that she had "heard that a time or two."

Annie had to smile at the way Winnie was clearly taking charge of the little band of friends. She was just as open and cheerful as could be and the others willingly deferred to her outgoing personality.

"Betty Lou brought you some homemade bread," Winnie continued earnestly, "and I brought along a couple of jars of my strawberry preserves. I'm not much of a baker, not like these gals or your Grandma Abby. No, I'm more inclined to canning and preserves myself. I have quite a large strawberry patch in my backyard." Winnie paused mid-sentence, catching the looks on Lillian and Betty Lou's faces that told her she was rambling on. "But I can tell you all about that another time," she said quickly with a nod to the two smiling women.

"How was your trip?" Lillian asked as they followed Annie into the kitchen, and each took a seat around the kitchen table as Annie put the kettle on for tea. "It was a long flight," Annie replied a moment later as she took her seat, reaching for one of the deliciously aromatic cinnamon buns the older woman had brought, "but it was otherwise uneventful."

"Just how I like my flights," Betty Lou piped in, "uneventful."

"Is there anything you need that you haven't been able to find?" Lillian asked Annie.

"Nothing I can think of at the moment," Annie replied. "But to be honest, I haven't gone shopping, yet. I am just catching up on sleep and exploring the property. It's been a long time since I was in this house—everything looks smaller." The women laughed at her observation, so common when revisiting childhood memories. "I guess my perspective was a bit lower when I was eight" she concluded with a smile.

"Well dear, we know you have a lot to do," Lillian said to Annie, rising to her feet a short while later.

"If there's anything you need, don't you hesitate to let us know, you hear? We've lived in this town all of our lives and there isn't much that goes on around here that we don't know about," Winnie assured Annie as they said their good-byes.

She was sure Winnie meant that last statement to be reassuring, but Annie found it comical, not to mention stereotypical, in its reference to old ladies knowing everyone's business. She smiled and waved from the front porch as she watched Winnie back her huge yellow car out of the driveway without so much as a backward glance. I guess when yours is the only house on the lane, you don't have to worry about oncoming traffic. Something else Annie would have to adjust to now that she no longer lived in the city. "I suppose I can get used to that," Annie said aloud as she turned and walked back into the house, eager to continue exploring her new home.

CHAPTER 4

Annie rose early and came downstairs to put on the kettle. She never used to drink hot tea in the morning, but it had become her habit since arriving in Magnolia Creek a little over two weeks ago, and now it just felt right somehow in this place, in her grandmother's kitchen. The thought made her smile to herself, remembering her grandmother's morning greeting.

Wiping her hands on her apron, her grandmother would say, "Good morning, Sunshine," and then ask, "so what will it be this morning? Eggs and bacon? Biscuits and jam? Or, are you in the mood for pot roast?"

Every morning it was the same greeting. Annie's response was always, "Pot roast, of course!" They would laugh together over their silly joke and Grandma Abby would ask her how she slept and what her plans were for the day. Annie loved the easy conversation and special attention she always received from her grandmother.

Annie carried her freshly brewed tea to the worn kitchen table and sat down. A big pewter water pitcher sat in the middle of the kitchen table and had been filled with fresh flowers for as long as Annie could remember. At the moment, the pitcher was empty as the tulips had died off and it was still too early for daisies. During the holidays the pitcher was removed and the matching bowl was filled with fresh apples, cinnamon-scented pinecones or festive ornaments, and cinnamon sticks tied with ribbon. Annie made a mental note to buy some fresh flowers. The sight of the empty pitcher was depressing.

Suddenly, there was a knock at the door. She hadn't even heard a car pull up.

"We thought you might like some fresh flowers to spruce up the place a bit," Betty Lou said as Annie opened the front door to her knock. "Your grandmother's summer flowers will be blooming soon enough and you'll have plenty to spare, but until then, we thought you might enjoy a bit of the outdoors right here on the kitchen table. There's just nothing like fresh flowers to brighten up a room."

"You must have been reading my mind," Annie said, happily accepting the bouquet of flowers Betty Lou handed her. "I was just thinking the same thing."

"So how are you getting along, Annie? Are you settling in and finding everything okay?" Lillian asked as they took their seats around the kitchen table while Annie poured tea. "Oh, before I forget it again. I've been meaning to invite you to come to church with us on Sunday. Your grandmother was a fixture at that old church and I just know you'll like it there, too."

"That sounds great," Annie said enthusiastically. "Count me in."

As they sat at the old kitchen table drinking their tea, Annie asked the women about her grandmother, explaining that she only knew Grandma Abby from a child's perspective. She wanted to know what was she like as a woman and a friend. Annie felt very comfortable talking with these women, and they knew her grandmother best.

She sensed that it was important to them as well that she learn about Abby Porter Smith. That's how these women thought of Abby, by her maiden and married name since they had known each other all their lives. Abby and Lillian had been in the same class all through school and had been neighbors with the other two who were a grade behind them. Their husbands had all gone to school together, as had their children.

As they each took turns telling her about her grandmother, Annie came to understand that Abby had a way about her that was a sort of quiet strength. She was kind and compassionate and was regularly involved in church and community activities. During church suppers or potluck dinners, they told her that Abby could always be found standing over the stove in the big kitchen or organizing the room setup for the tables and chairs. She baked bread and cookies for the bake sales, visited the sick in the hospital and the elderly in their homes. She was as much a part of the community as it was of her.

Abby had been raised in Magnolia Creek, had married her high school sweetheart shortly after graduation, and she and Ben had raised their daughter in the same house they moved into when they were first married. Abby loved her house and what she referred to as her seven acres of heaven. Ben had built the greenhouse for her a few years before he passed. He said he knew how much Abby's flowers meant to her and he wanted her to be able to enjoy them all year.

Annie enjoyed her visits with her grandmother's friends and she looked forward to those hours they would come and keep her company in that big house. Lillian worried that they may be wearing out their welcome by stopping by two or three times a week, but the truth was that Annie enjoyed their company. She had only been in town a couple of weeks and she was keeping busy around the house, but she was starting to feel lonely. With all of her friends and family across the country, Annie was grateful for the ladies' attention.

"So, we'll see you at church on Sunday morning?" Lillian reminded Annie as she and Betty Lou prepared to leave.

"Absolutely," Annie replied. "I'm looking forward to it."

CHAPTER 5

Shortly before church the next Sunday, as Annie helped Betty Lou set up for the luncheon on the lawn, she heard someone behind her exclaim, "Annie Reed! I heard you were in town, but I just couldn't believe it!"

Annie turned to find a young woman, about her own age, standing behind her holding a toddler with one hand and a young girl with the other. She was smiling broadly and hurrying toward Annie. As Annie started to say hello, the young woman reached out and pulled her into a big hug. "I can't believe you're back after all these years! It is so good to see you, Annie."

"Becca Tinsdale?" Annie said slowly as she recognized her old friend. She and Annie had been inseparable since their first day of school. "Becca Tinsdale, oh my gosh, how are you?"

"It's Jameson now—Becca Jameson. Scott and I got married right after high school so it'll be ten years this summer. You probably don't remember Scott," Becca continued, "I think you had already left when his family moved here. And these are my kids; Angela is eight, and Drew just turned four." Becca paused for a moment. "It's hard to believe that we were just Angela's age when you left. I still remember it clearly."

"So do I," Annie commiserated, "it was torture!"

Becca's family had moved into a house on the street behind Annie's just a few days before school started. For the next four years, they walked to school together each day and had sleepovers as often as they were allowed. Although Becca had an older brother, neither one had any sisters so they became inseparable, at least until she moved away. Annie had planned to look up Becca after she got settled but that hadn't happened yet. She was busier now than when she first arrived.

"So tell me about you," Becca urged as she pulled up a chair and sat down. Angela and Drew noticed some of their friends arriving and ran off to play. Annie looked around for Betty Lou as she had promised to help her set up for the luncheon after the service. It was such a beautiful day they had decided to eat outside.

She found Betty Lou busy giving directions to several teenaged boys who had just arrived to help. Annie caught her eye and saw Betty Lou smile with understanding. She winked and nodded at Annie and returned her attention to wrangling the boys into focusing on the task at hand, and not on the teenaged girls in their Sunday dresses. It would take every ounce of concentration Betty Lou had, but she loved every minute of it.

Annie told her about her life after leaving Magnolia Creek, catching her up on twenty years of history in a few moments. It was enough for now. She was sure they would find the time to catch up on the details. After all, Annie was back to stay.

"So you never married?" Becca asked her pointedly.

"No," Annie replied, "not yet anyway. Right now I am focusing on settling into this new phase of my life and figuring out my next steps."

As the church bells announced the start of morning services a few moments later, Annie and Becca made their way inside having already made plans to get together the following Saturday.

It really is starting to feel like home, Annie thought to herself as she took her seat between Lillian and Betty Lou. Life is good, she thought as she smiled warmly at her new friends.

CHAPTER 6

As she sat drinking her coffee, Annie thought about the plan she and Becca had made to clean out the attic today. By now it was a beautiful day with sunny skies and a soft breeze. It was a perfect day to open the windows and let in the fresh air. As she went around the downstairs opening windows, Annie let her mind wander to what mysteries she might uncover in the attic today. She had been looking forward to this day with anticipation. Annie wasn't exactly sure what she would uncover up there under all that dust, but she was sure she would learn something new about her grandmother and her life in Magnolia Creek.

She returned to the kitchen to wait for Becca to arrive and was struck by the smell of soft spring flowers on the breeze coming through the living room windows and the sun that was shining warmly in the kitchen beyond. She poured another cup of coffee and thought about her grandmother sitting on the porch with an apron full of beans she was cleaning, tossing them into the pot on the table beside her. She could hear the crack and feel the fuzz of the green beans as her grandmother taught her how to snap off both ends without crushing the bean inside. A few moments later, she heard the screen door close, announcing Becca's arrival.

Becca had offered to help Annie clean out the attic and Annie had readily agreed. She believed this was going to be an emotional undertaking for Annie so she arranged for Scott to take the kids to the amusement park in Richmond so she and Annie would have all day together. She arrived at eight o'clock as they had agreed, dressed in a worn-out pair of blue jeans and one of Scott's old college sweatshirts.

"Good morning, sunshine," Becca called out cheerfully as she entered the bright and sunny kitchen.

Annie had been lost in her thoughts staring out the kitchen windows when Becca arrived. "Good morning," Annie replied, turning to give Becca a hug. "You're in good spirits this morning."

"I should be," Becca replied. "Scott and the kids left two hours ago to get to the park before it opens so I was able to sleep in for a change."

"Well I made a full pot of coffee and I have some of Lillian's fabulous cinnamon rolls if you're interested. That should give us quite a jumpstart this morning." Annie laughed, referring to the large quantities of sugar that no doubt had been mixed with equally large quantities of butter to make the rolls melt in your mouth.

"God bless you!" Becca replied with enthusiasm. "I am trying to set a good example for my kids to eat healthy, but in this case what they don't know won't hurt them."

They sat together at the kitchen table quietly anticipating the day ahead while they enjoyed their cinnamon rolls and coffee. Annie appreciated her old friend so much in that moment that she was moved to reach out and squeeze her hand. Becca smiled knowingly at her and squeezed back. Neither of them knew exactly what to expect, but they did know this was going to be a day that would stir up memories for Annie and perhaps even uncover new information about her family.

"Well, my friend," Becca said practically as she rose from the table, "that attic is just not going to clean itself."

Annie smiled at her friend's enthusiasm and joined her in clearing the table.

"I really appreciate this," Annie said sincerely to Becca, "and…"

Becca held up her hand to stop her from continuing. "Listen, Annie," she began as she reached out to take Annie's hands, "I can only imagine how hard this is for you. I remember how close you and your grandmother were when you lived here and I know this is bringing back memories for you, being in this house and knowing she's gone." Annie nodded silently with tears slowly beginning to roll down her face. "I'm here for you, my friend. We are going to do this together, and when you need to take a break you just say the word, okay?"

Annie nodded, took a deep breath, and said, "I'm ready." They turned and headed for the stairs.

Annie paused before she started up the stairs to the attic. "Are you sure you're ready for this?" Becca asked with concern as she took Annie's elbow to steady her. "There's no reason to rush."

Annie turned to smile at her childhood friend and replied, "Yes, I'm sure. I just thought this would be another adventure and I've really been looking forward to it. So why am I nervous about going up there?"

"It's not nerves," Becca explained with a straight face, "it's the pound of butter from the cinnamon rolls clogging your arteries and the two cups of sugar making your heart race. Don't worry"—she smiled at Annie, starting up the stairs ahead of her friend—"if you can make it up the stairs, you're home free."

Becca's humor was just what Annie needed. She climbed the stairs after her friend, stopping beside her when they reached the top.

"The first thing we're going to do," Becca said, "is see if we can get a few of these dormer windows open to get some ventilation in here and clear out some of the dust."

As they went about that task, Annie was calmed by the fact that the boxes, trunks, and miscellaneous items that she could not yet identify were all arranged fairly neatly, allowing access to even the furthest corners of the attic. When they'd managed to get a couple of the windows open, the breeze seemed to carry out the smells of old papers, dust, and leather while bringing in smells of fresh air and early summer flowers. It was a welcome relief and the soothing smells of her grandmother's flowers calmed Annie's nerves.

....

They set about the task of opening boxes and trunks first. There were stacks of boxes that held Abby's treasured memories. Boxes of pictures, scrapbooks, and what looked like her mother's schoolwork. There were trunks of clothing that appeared to have belonged to her grandparents when they were younger, mostly formal clothing like suits and fancy dresses. Many of the boxes contained paperwork and ledgers from what appeared to be her grandfather's businesses.

As she and Becca continued their work, they chatted about their lives, their families, and memories they had from those early years when they could not imagine a time when they would not be together. After a couple of hours of slowly going through each box and sorting its contents, Annie stood up to take a break. As she walked toward one of the open windows, something caught her eye. A glint of sunlight reflected off something shiny in the far corner. Her first glance told here there were only boxes that appeared to be filled with financial records. Yet something had drawn her gaze. She made her way to the far corner of the attic where there were boxes stacked four and five rows high and at least three rows deep.

To the left of the rows of boxes, nearest to the wall, stood a large cheval mirror and a dressmaker's mannequin with what appeared to be a gown covered by plastic and a large black drape. The drape had been blown open by the breeze from the open windows. As Annie drew closer, she reached out to lift the drape for a better look and discovered that inside was a white, silk gown that had small, white daisies with gold sequin centers embroidered into the fabric of the bodice and train.

It was her grandmother's wedding gown. She had seen that dress hundreds of times as she went up the stairs to bed each night. For as long as Annie could remember, her mother had hung family photos on the wall going up the stairs. The photo she remembered was in black and white so until now she never knew the center of the daisies were gold.

She stood and stared at that dress for several minutes before reaching out to touch it. This discovery moved her more than anything else they had uncovered in the attic so far. It connected her with her Grandma Abby on a personal level and she could not take her eyes off the intricate detailing of the stitching, the way the sequins caught the light, and the smooth silkiness of the gown itself. It was incredible.

Annie found herself wondering if it would fit.

CHAPTER 7

"C'mon, girl," Annie called to Daisy as she bounded out of Winnie's big, yellow car and headed for the front porch. Annie was sure she was about to be knocked over by the lumbering Golden Retriever as she raced across the front yard. A moment later, Daisy veered suddenly to the right and headed for the hedgerow that ran along the north side of the house and into the backyard.

"Saying hello to your friends, I see," Annie said to Daisy as she headed right for the spot where Annie had seen a large cottontail rabbit not two hours before. Daisy sniffed enthusiastically for a few moments then turned and ran to the large maple tree in the corner of the front yard. As she circled it with her nose to the ground, the two squirrels that had entertained Annie for the last few weeks watched Daisy closely and chided her vigorously for interrupting their play. The large dog barked purposefully at them, paused long enough to mark her territory, and made a beeline for Annie.

"Well it took you long enough," Annie chided Daisy as she braced for impact. It was a good thing she did, too, or the large dog would surely have toppled her over as she circled Annie, rubbing against her legs forcefully in an attempt to get as close as possible. When Daisy's head came around where Annie could reach it, she grabbed her affectionately, scratched behind her ears, and gave her a big kiss.

"I'd say it's a tie as to who is happier that Daisy's home," Winnie said cheerfully to Annie as she made her way up the walk to the front porch.

"It's hard to believe, but I couldn't wait for her to get here," Annie said to Winnie with wonder in her voice. "I never had a pet of my own, but I feel like Daisy's been my dog all my life. How can that be?"

"I imagine it's because your Grandma Abby had a dog just like her when you were a little girl. In fact, this Daisy is actually your Daisy's great-granddaughter," Winnie explained, "so, I don't think it's strange at all that you feel connected to her so quickly. Then again, at my age I don't find much strange anymore."

"How about some iced tea?" Winnie asked Annie as she opened the screen door and let herself inside.

"That sounds wonderful," Annie said, "but I can get it. There's some already made in the pitcher in the fridge."

"You don't need to wait on me," Winnie piped up. "You two come in and let Daisy get reacquainted with the place while I fix our drinks."

Annie carried the bag of Daisy's belongings into the house and immediately set out her bowls, filling one with water before she sat it down. She knew that when Daisy was finished making her rounds, she'd be looking for it. It was good to have her home.

The truth was that Annie would have loved to bring Daisy home right away, but Winnie and the ladies had encouraged her to take a little time to get settled before taking on the additional responsibility of a dog. In hindsight, she had to agree with them. Annie had never owned a dog and she took full advantage of learning how to care for Daisy while she was temporarily living with Winnie. Annie learned all about her feeding, grooming, and outdoor schedule so she would be ready for anything when she brought her home. At least that's what she thought.

It took Daisy no time at all to readjust to being in her own home after staying with Winnie for nearly three months. By the time Winnie said good-bye a short time later, Daisy was sleeping comfortably on the floor at Annie's feet with her favorite toy firmly lodged in her mouth. Annie felt more at home now than she had since she'd arrived. It was a match made in heaven.

CHAPTER 8

They were enjoying an evening of storytelling and knitting at Annie's house when Betty Lou first noticed how pale Lillian looked. She acted like she was feeling fine, so Betty Lou just made a mental note to keep an eye on her but did not mention it to anyone else. After all, she may just be unnecessarily cautious about her friend's health so soon after losing Abby.

As the evening progressed, Lillian became quieter and less responsive to the conversation. Betty Lou discreetly caught Winnie's eye and tilted her head toward Lillian. Winnie turned her attention toward Lillian as she continued her discussion with Annie. She realized that Lillian was not fully following the conversation and appeared to be staring into space. Annie picked up on the exchange between Winnie and Betty Lou and quietly rose from her chair and announced she was going into the kitchen to make more tea. She could tell by their actions that they did not want to alarm Lillian.

"Winnie," she asked pointedly, looking at each woman in turn, "would you mind putting the kettle on while Betty Lou and I put out some cookies?" When they looked at her, she glanced at Lillian and inclined her head in the direction of the kitchen. Each woman played along and got slowly to their feet, careful not to disturb Lillian's gaze. They needn't have bothered with the charade, Lillian never even blinked.

"What should we do?" Annie asked, all pretenses dropped when they met in the kitchen. "Has she been like this before?"

"No," Winnie and Betty Lou both replied solemnly and shook their heads.

"I think we need to call Dr. Morrison," Winnie stated with certainty, Betty Lou nodding her agreement.

A quick call was placed to Lillian's family doctor and as his service tried to reach him, the women returned to the living room to check on Lillian. By this time she was unresponsive and still staring into space. Worried, the women looked at each other and knew that they needed to call for an ambulance. As Annie reached for the phone, it rang.

After receiving Annie's description of Lillian's symptoms, Dr. Morrison instructed them to call 911 immediately and he would meet them at the hospital.

They made the drive to the hospital in silence, following the ambulance as closely as they could as it made its way into town, lights flashing steadily. They had decided to take Winnie's car so they could all ride together. Normally cheerful and chatty, Winnie was navigating the roads to the hospital in silence, focused as they all were on praying for their friend.

By the time the women arrived at the hospital, parked, and got inside, Dr. Morrison was already ordering tests and conferring with the attending physician. As they kept vigil in the waiting room, Dr. Morrison would periodically appear to give them updates on Lillian's condition. With the exception of Annie, he had known all of them for more years than he could count. He had also been Abby's doctor, so he was sensitive to what the friends were going through at the moment.

After several hours and many tests, they learned that Lillian had suffered a stroke. She was stable, but it was serious.

Early the next morning as Lillian was being moved into a room on the cardiac floor of the hospital, the women took the opportunity to go home to freshen up. Winnie and Betty Lou dropped Annie off first, and they agreed to meet her at the hospital again in a couple of hours.

Annie was worried about Lillian. And not just because of her physical condition. When Lillian first became ill, Annie jumped into action. She knew the emotional toll a serious illness would have on her new friend, especially so soon after losing Abby. Lillian, Winnie, and Betty Lou had done so much for Annie and she wanted desperately to find a way to do something nice for Lillian. To show her appreciation in some small way. To show Lillian how much she cared about her. She thought immediately of her grandmother's flowers.

She would make the biggest and most beautiful bouquet she could manage. She may not be able to do much for her friend, but she could at least attempt to brighten her day. It was a start.

It took Annie over an hour to make the arrangement, but it was worth it. She was proud of her creation and she knew that Lillian would love it. She was right.

Annie returned to the hospital shortly after ten that morning and was told that Lillian had been moved to a private room on the third floor. Room 309 was a fairly small room with a window at one end and a recliner for when Lillian felt up to getting out of bed. Two additional visitor chairs had been squeezed into the compact room, and Winnie and Betty Lou occupied both of them.

Lillian was awake and sipping from her straw when Annie's bouquet preceded her into the room. All three women marveled at the gorgeous arrangement and Winnie cleared a place on the small shelf under the television that was mounted above. "That way," she explained, "Lillian can see the beautiful flowers each time she opens her eyes."

"They are so beautiful, Annie," Lillian said with tears welling up in her eyes. She reached for Annie's hand and looked her in the eye. "Thank you."

Annie was deeply moved by Lillian's reaction. Winnie and Betty Lou also had tears in their eyes, looking at Annie as if she had brought the most wonderful gift they had ever seen.

"It was no problem," Annie explained cheerfully in an attempt to lighten the mood in the room. "I just thought you would like something to look at besides wires and tubes."

Having not known her grandmother well, she had no way of knowing that bringing Lillian a handmade bouquet of her favorite flowers was exactly what her Grandma Abby would have done.

The next couple of hours were spent discussing the events of the night before, what might happen next, what all the tubes and wires actually did, and finally taking bets on what would be under the dome of her lunch tray. They decided it was time to let Lillian get some rest. As they said good-bye to Lillian and assured her they would be back later that afternoon, she hugged each one of them in turn.

When she came to Annie, she held her close. "When you arrived with those flowers, I thought for a moment that Abby had returned to me. You are so like her, my dear. Bringing me those flowers is exactly what she would have done. As much joy as flowers brought to her, Abby also understood the joy they brought to others, especially those in need of cheering up. God bless you, my dear. God bless you real good," Lillian said with a warm smile and a pat on her hand. "Now you go home and get some rest, you hear? I'll be fine. It's not like I'm going to be lonely with those nurses in here waking me up every hour to poke or prod something!"

Annie left with Winnie and Betty Lou, confident that her friend was in good hands and good spirits. The truth was, she was exhausted.

CHAPTER 9

Dr. Anderson, Lillian's cardiologist, was a tall, slender man with a kind face and bright-blue eyes. He spoke softly and made a point to take Lillian's hand each time he spoke with her. The women had met him on several occasions, and he always greeted them warmly, thanking them for taking such good care of his favorite patient.

Lillian had been in the hospital and under Dr. Anderson's care for a week now. On this particular morning, after greeting them each by name, he asked the women to excuse them so he could speak to Lillian alone. Annie was just standing up to leave when Lillian informed him that these women were family and she wanted them to stay. As he looked around the room at each of them, his face broke into a smile and when he turned back to Lillian, he nodded and took her hand.

"I'm afraid the news is not what you had hoped for, Lillian," he explained gently. "You need to be around people who can care for you and keep a close watch on your medications. Therefore, I am recommending that you be placed in a full time care facility. I know you were hoping to go home soon, Lillian, and I'm sorry to tell you that is not an option." He paused and allowed Lillian and her friends to grasp what he had told them. When no questions were forthcoming, he offered helpfully, "I do know of a wonderful place nearby that is currently accepting residents. They've converted the old high school into an assisted living facility and they named it Magnolia Lane. If you'd like I can have one of my staff stop by with a brochure for you to look at. I'm sure you would like it there and they have an excellent program. I wouldn't normally recommend a place so highly, but my own mother has been a resident there for the past five months. In my opinion, it has lived up to its promises. Please let me know if you have any questions, Lillian. I'll stop in to check on you again tomorrow morning."

Magnolia Lane used to be the high school, before the new combination middle school and high school was built on the outskirts of town. It was a clever design for a nursing facility, with wide hallways and large windows in every room. The ceilings were high and the light fixtures were beautiful antiques. The rooms were large and provided enough space to fit two residents to a room. Closets and bathrooms had been added and the rooms were designed to provide a small common sitting area. The design also ensured that each resident had a window view and privacy if they wished. The privacy curtains could come in very handy when one's roommate liked to turn her light on at all hours.

At least that's what Lillian's roommate did. Eva could be so irritating at times and be just as sweet as pie at other times. She had a way of getting under Lillian's skin and that's exactly what she had been doing lately. Since her granddaughter's visit the previous weekend, Eva had been irritable and sullen.

Lillian had tried talking to her many times, to no avail. Eva was just not in the mood. *Well, if that's the way she wants it, that's fine with me,* Lillian thought. She knew how to mind her own business and that's just what she intended to do. Eva could just sit over there and stew in her own juices for all she cared.

Lillian knew the reason for her roommate's mood but she could do nothing to help her if Eva wouldn't talk to her about it. Eva's granddaughter Rachel and her husband Paul came to see her last weekend to tell her it was time to sell her house. It's too much work for them to maintain with their own house and family to take care of. There were repairs needed and just maintaining the outside grounds was proving too much for Paul. He had resorted to hiring a neighborhood boy to do the mowing, but that was not a long-term solution. The house needed to be lived in. It was a beautiful old house with old being the operative word. It needed constant care and maintenance and Paul just did not have that kind of free time.

Lillian supposed that Eva had been struggling with the certainty that she would never again return to her home. Lillian knew the challenge Eva was facing was depression. She needed a reason to go on and not give up on life. She wished she could help her new friend, but Eva was moody and difficult. Lillian had been as patient as possible, but it was wearing on her. After all, she was in the same situation. Lillian understood that she needed to keep a positive outlook and she chose to be grateful for the opportunity to live in Magnolia Lane. Having her friends around certainly helped her to stay positive. While it was hard to see them leave each day and return to their homes, her acceptance of her situation helped her to feel more at home in Magnolia Lane and she began to think of this room as her home. When she stopped to think about it, Lillian realized that she was actually enjoying having a roommate. At least she was until a week ago, but Eva's pessimistic attitude was making it increasingly difficult.

If we live long enough, Lillian thought, *we all must face our own mortality. For many of us, the loss of independence may be one of the biggest hurdles to overcome on the path to acceptance.* She sounded like the Dalai Lama. She smiled to herself. But it was true. Lillian had been struggling with that very issue for several months now. She thought for a moment that if she were entirely honest with herself, she had been struggling with it for much longer than that.

Since Bill died nearly fifteen years ago, Lillian had been forced to face the hard truth that she was not as young as she used to be and could not continue to act as if she was. Bill had taken care of everything when he was alive. Oh, she knew how to pay the bills and handle her finances, but she was hopelessly over her head when it came to taking care of the house or the car or even, it seemed, getting the trash to the curb on time.

She still missed him. They had been married for fifty-two years and had raised two wonderful sons. Her first thought was of Charlie, the eldest of her sons, living happily in Atlanta with his family. Then there was James. They'd lost poor James when he was just nineteen. Bill had been so proud when his youngest son had joined the army to serve his country, and it had just about broken his heart when he died.

But that was such a long time ago, now. They both held a very special place in her heart, but Lillian had been forced to move on and keep living, which was exactly what she was doing now. She knew how precious each day was and had decided long ago not to waste a single one.

She would have to pray about how best to help Eva, Lillian decided. She would lay it at God's feet and He would guide her in her heart just as He had always done. Lillian smiled to herself as a sense of peace came over her.

CHAPTER 10

"Is that the last of the boxes?" Annie heard someone shout through the front door. "I think that's it," Annie replied as she scanned the empty living room. Becca's husband Scott came through the door a moment later, wiping sweat from his brow. He had spent most of the morning packing the rented trailer with those of Lillian's belongings that she had decided to keep. Most of the boxes would end up in the small storage room that Grandpa Ben had built in what had now become Annie's barn. The furniture and small appliances that Lillian had not already given away to her friends and neighbors had been donated to various charities earlier in the week.

As Scott headed into the kitchen to let Becca know he was ready to go, Annie took a moment to look around the room, thinking about how much had happened in the past few weeks.

Annie was struck by a sense of loss. As she stood in the middle of the room and looked around, she felt she understood more clearly the sense of loss that Lillian must be dealing with, knowing she would never again return to her home. The home she and Bill built together and where they had raised their sons. Annie's move had been an upheaval of her life, to be sure, but she had made a conscious choice to follow her heart. She had stepped into her new future based on a strong sense of faith that the move was part of God's plan for her life. She prayed that Lillian had the benefit of that same sense of faith with her move.

"Well, the kitchen is done and clean," Becca said brightly as she came out of the kitchen and headed toward Annie, wiping her hands on an old kitchen towel. Annie didn't respond and appeared to be lost in thought. "Annie," Becca asked gently, putting her hand on her friend's shoulder. "Are you okay?"

"It just seems so final, doesn't it?" Annie asked Becca with tears welling up in her eyes. "I mean, I know Lillian has lived a long and full life, but one day she's standing in her kitchen baking cinnamon buns and the next thing you know she's leaving her home, never to return. How do you suppose she is able to deal with that so calmly? Honestly, I think I'm more upset than she is."

"I don't know," Becca replied honestly, giving her friend a reassuring hug. "Maybe her perspective is a little different than ours."

"How do you mean?" Annie asked, wiping her eyes as she stood back to look at her friend.

"Well, we see this as a loss, right? Maybe Lillian sees this as just another chapter in her life. Or even a new adventure," Becca said, warming up to the idea that there could be a way to see this event in a positive light.

"How exactly is moving into a nursing home an adventure?" Annie asked skeptically.

"Oh, I don't know," Becca said, shrugging her shoulders slightly, thinking about how to answer Annie's question. "Maybe she's looking forward to meeting new people, having a roommate, not eating alone or even having regular activities she can participate in. Perhaps Lillian doesn't see the freedom and appeal that we see when we think of living on our own.

"At her age, Lillian may see that very independence that we treasure as lonely or even a bit scary. She may live with an underlying fear of taking a bad fall or forgetting to turn off the oven. There may be any number of things we take for granted that cause her worry when there is no one around to help. We just don't think like that at our age."

"Maybe you're right," Annie said thoughtfully. "It certainly would explain why she is so accepting of her circumstances. I mean, I know that it's a change for her and change can be scary, but she and the ladies certainly are handling the whole affair much better than I am. Then again, perhaps they're all putting on brave faces for each other as well as for me."

"There's always that," Becca said with a grin, seeing her friend's mood improve as she thought of the finely honed skills those seemingly harmless old ladies had when it came to getting others to do what they thought was best for them. Annie herself had been "played" on more than one occasion.

CHAPTER 11

When Dr. Anderson told them that Lillian was going into a nursing home, Annie feared that she would give up hope and lose her will to live. She knew that it would be easy for Lillian to become lonely and despondent. After all, it would be a big lifestyle change for her and her friends. She supposed they could still stop over for tea and visit with Lillian, but she was not in a private room and did not have her own kitchen to prepare the tea.

Although Annie had no control over Lillian's living arrangements, she certainly could do her part to make her comfortable and feel at home there. She vowed that day to visit Lillian at least twice a week.

Annie felt better already. She remembered when her Grandpa Reed had a stroke and went into a nursing home. Annie went with her mother to sit with him for a few hours on Saturday mornings. Annie was around seven years old at the time and she could remember feeling sad that he was sick, afraid that he would die, and guilty because she did not want to go. The smell was the worst part. Now that she thought about it, she could still remember that smell. Her mother had explained that it was just cleaning solution but Annie thought it smelled like sadness.

Grandpa Reed never came home again. He passed away a few months after entering the nursing home. As an adult, Annie knew that he had suffered from the effects of the stroke, but as a child, she was convinced he'd died of sadness.

Annie was true to her word and visited Lillian at least twice a week. She brought her friend books and magazines to read, and sometimes she even brought a small puzzle or a game to play if Lillian felt up to it.

Annie hadn't given much thought to growing flowers since she and her parents had moved away from Magnolia Creek when she was just a child. Before that time, flowers seemed to be a part of her everyday existence. She spent a lot of time with her grandmother and they spent most of their time together tending to the outdoor flowerbeds in the warm months and tending to the greenhouse plants during the colder months. Annie and her mother had attempted to plant and grow flowers in the backyard of her new home but it just wasn't the same without Grandma Abby. Eventually Annie became involved with new friends and school activities and that part of her life became a warm but faded memory.

Moving back here changed all of that. It was as if she had stepped back in time. Although her grandmother was no longer with her, the love for Grandma Abby's flowers and the joy she felt tending to them and arranging the cut blooms for vases in the house made Annie feel as if a part of her grandmother was still there. After Lillian had moved into the assisted living facility earlier that summer, Annie found a way to bring that joy to others and keep doing what she loved.

It began simply enough when she took the first bouquet to Lillian as a gift to brighten up her new room. Annie vowed to bring Lillian a new bouquet each week to do her part to keep Lillian's spirits up, and it had worked beautifully. Annie was surprised to find that other residents looked forward to her weekly deliveries as much as Lillian did. In fact, it became a popular activity on the second floor to take a planned yet seemingly casual stroll by Lillian's room on Saturday morning to see the latest creation Annie brought. Lillian suggested at one point that they could sell tickets, although Annie knew she was happy to have the visitors.

After talking with the staff, Annie realized that there were several residents who were completely alone. They had no family, or none in the area, and never received visits or gifts. *Every life is a gift from God,* Annie thought, *and every life deserved to be celebrated.* Annie knew right away that she was being called into service to somehow help these people who had no one else. From that day on, she always managed to have a few extra flowers with her that she left with the staff to give to those lonely souls who needed them most. There is just something so cheerful about fresh cut flowers. One of the staff members had even bought glass vases for each recipient, hand painted with their names and favorite flowers.

It wasn't long before they told Annie that the residents who received the flowers were anxious to thank her in person. She began to visit with each of them every week when she delivered their flowers. She took the time to read to some, write letters for others, and just listen to those who had no one to hear their stories. She loved spending her Saturday mornings at Magnolia Lane and looked forward to her visits with people she now considered family.

Annie soon realized she was going to run out of flowers before the end of the summer. The greenhouse would help for a few months, but it wasn't a large building and was never intended to produce flowers on this scale. No, she would have to find another way. She would not consider cutting back on her deliveries, knowing how much both she and the residents enjoyed her visits and the fresh flowers.

Even before she realized what she was doing, Annie began mentally listing the pros and cons of opening her own flower shop in Magnolia Creek. She could buy the flowers wholesale and the profits from the shop would easily pay for the donations she made each week to the residents of Magnolia Lane. She had been thinking that she needed to find something to do with her life, and the more she thought about it, the more sense it made to her. She would have to give this new idea some serious thought.

CHAPTER 12

"I'm so glad Daisy is back home where she belongs and that Annie has taken to her so well," Lillian told her friends. "I worried that with all the change in her life recently, Annie wouldn't want to add a pet to the mix, especially not one as energetic as Daisy."

"It's just so fitting, don't you think?" Betty Lou asked. "After all, Abby always had a Daisy, even when Annie was a little girl. It just wouldn't be the same without her."

"That's for sure," Winnie chimed in. "It just wouldn't be right."

The three of them were enjoying a nice afternoon on the patio at Magnolia Lane, soaking up the spring sunshine and enjoying the tall mint juleps the staff served on the patio. It made the ladies feel like southern belles. Ladies of leisure drinking their mint juleps, discussing the love of their family and friends, and occasionally plotting ways to "help" those they decided needed their particular brand of help. Annie was the recipient of their scheming today and in all honesty, she was their favorite beneficiary.

"We need to find her a man," Betty Lou announced, much to the surprise of her two closest friends.

"What?" Winnie sputtered, surprised by the force of Betty Lou's words.

"What do you propose we do?" Lillian asked her calmly, glancing at Winnie to be sure she had recovered from her shock.

"Where in heaven's name did that come from?" Winnie had been so surprised by Betty Lou's uncharacteristically candid statement that she actually spilled her mint julep down the front of her blouse and into her lap.

When Winnie regained her composure a moment later, Betty Lou spoke up. "Well, I don't know exactly," she answered, frowning at Winnie's lack of control, "but there must be something we can do. Annie is such a treasure and I just know that Abby's counting on us to help her adjust to life here. She deserves a good man to love her and a family to fill that big house. Wouldn't you agree?"

"Yes, of course," Lillian and Winnie replied in unison, warming up to the idea of Annie settling in and raising a family in Abby's old house.

"So who do we know that would be suitable? There must be someone from church, someone her age who comes from a good stable family, not someone who likes to party too much," Betty Lou offered.

"Or someone who works all the time," Lillian added with a frown.

"He has to be handy, too," Winnie suggested. "That old house will need a lot of upkeep."

"This may take some work to figure out," Betty Lou mused. "How about we make a list? Then we can keep our eyes on these young men to see what they're made of."

"Oh, and we can arrange 'chance meetings' with Annie to see if there is any chemistry between them," Winnie interjected excitedly.

"If we play our cards right, we may be able to find her a suitable husband by Christmas. Wouldn't that be just perfect?" Betty Lou said wistfully.

"Wouldn't what be just perfect?" Annie asked as she came up behind Betty Lou and greeted her with a kiss on the cheek.

"Hello, dear," Lillian said, rising to greet Annie with a hug. "What brings you by? I thought you were spending the day with Becca and the kids. Wasn't today the trip to the zoo in Richmond?"

As Annie explained that Drew had woken up with a fever and stomach ache, Winnie just shook her head with wonder at now deftly Lillian had maneuvered the conversation away from Betty Lou, allowing her ample time to come up with a response to Annie's question. As Annie sat down and accepted the mint julep offered by an alert staffer, she repeated her question to Betty Lou.

"What would be just perfect?" Annie asked expectantly. "What are we talking about?" Knowing that Annie was smart enough to see through a flimsy cover story, Betty Lou knew her response had to be good if they were going to keep their undertaking a secret.

"Oh, we were just thinking how perfect it would be to have an old fashioned Christmas at your place this year. What do you think?" Gauging by the look on Annie's face, Betty Lou said quickly, "I know it seems a bit early to be making plans for Christmas, but there's no time like the present to starting the planning, right?"

"A bit early?" Annie asked incredulously. "It's the middle of May. We haven't even celebrated the Fourth of July and you're making plans for Christmas?" Annie looked around the table as they all smiled back at her.

"Now, Annie, these things take time and they don't plan themselves you know. And besides," Lillian continued as Annie started to object, "it's tradition. Abby has had a Christmas party for as long as I can remember. In fact, I don't think even one year has passed where there wasn't a party there, do you?" Lillian asked her cohorts, looking to them for support.

"No," they both mused, shaking their heads, "not one."

"Even the year Ben passed," Betty Lou added, "as hard as it was to get all the decorations up, Abby still had the Christmas party."

Annie looked at her hands in her lap, feeling bad that she had made such a big deal about something that obviously meant a lot to these women. She also recognized this would be the first Christmas without Grandma Abby. Annie missed her grandmother, but she knew that she didn't feel the pain of Abby's absence to the same extent as these women. They had been lifelong friends. As such, their lives would always seem to be missing something. She would have to try to remember that and be more understanding.

"Well, who am I to break tradition?" Annie asked with a reassuring smile. "Of course we'll have a Christmas party and it probably is a good idea to start planning early because I've never hosted a Christmas party before. Especially not one so steeped in tradition."

"It wasn't actually a lie," Betty Lou explained to Winnie over the phone later that evening. "Abby always did have a Christmas party, as did her parents before her. Even though, strictly speaking, it wasn't exactly what we were talking about when she walked up."

"Strictly speaking?" Winnie interjected. "It wasn't at all what we were talking about when she walked up!"

"I know, I know," Betty Lou said impatiently, "but I had to come up with something to tell her and I didn't have much time. We couldn't very well let her know about our 'secret mission' now could we?"

"Secret mission? What are you, some kind of spy? When did this happen, Betty Lou? Have you been watching too much TV again? Are you leading a double life? Oh, wait!" she exclaimed excitedly. "Are you a Russian spy who has been living here all your life just waiting for the call from the Motherland to activate your spy network?" Winnie laughed at her own mental picture of Betty Lou sneaking around stealing sensitive documents and clandestinely meeting men in trench coats and fedoras.

"Are you quite through, Winifred?" Betty Lou asked sternly.

"Da, comrade," she responded, which sent her into another fit of laughter so infectious that Betty Lou could not resist laughing herself.

"You're a horse's petute, Winifred Porter," Betty Lou said, now laughing openly with her friend.

CHAPTER 13

Tom felt like he could breathe here. It was literally a world away from L.A. and he couldn't be happier. He had been fortunate enough to find a wonderful house to rent and was able to help the landlady with odd jobs around the place. He loved working with his hands. That was something that his dad had never understood. In his mind you had to be moving and shaking to make your mark boldly and quickly in life. That was the key to real success, according to his father. Of course his father considered a man to be successful only when his accomplishments were very public and very profitable.

Tom found it hard to believe he was cut from the same cloth as his father. They could not be more different. If he was honest with himself, from an early age Tom had known that following in his father's footsteps was not for him. As much as he wanted to emulate his father and earn his praise, at his core Tom was much more concerned with relationships than money. He wanted to do something or build something tangible, something that actually helped people who needed it.

When he was seven, Tom organized a project at his school to collect pencils for underprivileged children he had heard about from visiting missionaries. The stories they told of children using sticks to write in the hard-packed dirt because they didn't have pencils or paper had touched him deeply. He went home that afternoon and gathered pens and pencils from every drawer and desktop he found. He then went to each of the neighbors on his street and asked them to do the same.

One of his teachers told the pastor at his church and he approached Tom to thank him for his efforts and to encourage him to reach out to the parishioners as well. Tom didn't need any more encouragement than that to begin a campaign that ended up going to the school board, becoming a district-wide campaign. Within a few short months, Tom had enlisted the help of several of his classmates and their parents (his had been too busy to help) to collect forty-seven cartons of pencils and pens to send to the missionaries for distribution to those very children that needed them.

He remembered the feeling of pride in himself and his friends when he presented the donations to the grateful missionaries. His smile faded quickly when he remembered that neither of his parents attended the special event and, in fact, made only a passing mention of it at dinner. His father had actually said that if he applied himself in that manner to his studies, he was bound to make partner before he was thirty.

Seven-year-old Tom didn't have a clue what that meant, but if his father wanted him to work hard then that's what he would do. He loved his father and desperately sought his approval. It wasn't until much later in his life that Tom discovered that no matter what he did to please his father, it was never enough. So, he mused, he'd decided to please himself. By his account, it was working out very nicely.

CHAPTER 14

As Annie sat on her back porch in her grandmother's old rocking chair, she couldn't stop thinking about the flower shop. Everywhere she turned there seemed to be signs pointing her in that direction. Her accountant called to discuss investment opportunities, recommending that Annie invest her inheritance. She noticed that the only place in town to buy somewhat-fresh flowers was the supermarket. When she wanted to buy Lillian a special, preferably handmade gift for her new room, she had to wait until she and Becca took one of their shopping trips into Richmond to find what she was looking for. Becca did tell her there were several artists and potters in the area, but it would be summer before they put out their goods for sale at the local art shows and craft fairs.

Annie suddenly realized that this was an enormous step she was considering. Putting down roots by owning a home and property was one thing, but owning a business was something else entirely. The fact that she was even considering it this soon after moving to Magnolia Creek took Annie by surprise. The next emotion could only be described as fear.

Fear of the unknown was natural, she told herself, there was a lot at stake. After all, what did she know about running a business? Quite a lot, she recognized suddenly, thinking of the flower shop she worked at all through college. Carrie, the shop owner, had taken her under her wing and showed her the ropes. She taught her not just about the flowers, but also about what it took to run a business. From ordering stock to pricing, care of flowers, and marketing. The fact of the matter was, she realized, she was actually very qualified.

As if that weren't enough, an unexpected sight warmed her heart and gave her confirmation that this was what God intended for her to do. There, under the old live oak tree in the backyard, sat her grandmother's old watering can, abandoned and half buried under the natural mulch. It was the one Grandma Abby had used for as long as Annie could remember.

Annie smiled knowingly as she noticed the small daisy growing inside the watering can. It was blooming beautifully, right where it was planted. Not in a manicured flowerbed or a traditional pot in a greenhouse, but in that old watering can, speaking clearly to her.

Suddenly she realized that she couldn't stop smiling. Not even if she wanted to. The tears began to roll down her face as she realized that she felt connected to this place in a way she never expected. The sense of belonging overwhelmed her and she knew without a doubt that she was exactly where God intended her to be.

"Well," Annie said aloud, "if this is where He wants me, then this is where I belong. Like the daisy in the watering can, I'll bloom where I'm planted." Contemplating her next move, Annie stood suddenly and headed into the house to do what any young woman in her situation would do. She was going to call her mother.

CHAPTER 15

"Good morning," Tom said as he knocked softly and stepped through the open door to number 24 Magnolia Lane. Tom took note that each room had its own address, providing the residents a sense of home, he supposed. He was actually quite impressed with the facility so far. He had been here once before to meet Eva, Paul's mother in-law and his new landlady, but they had met in the common area on the first floor to discuss the rental agreement. This, however, was a social call.

Tom had been renting Eva's home for almost six weeks now and he was anxious to show her pictures of what he had done to the place. Eva had been apprehensive about a stranger living in her home, but after meeting Tom and talking to him about his plans, she agreed that it would be a good idea to have a handyman there to take care of the place. She would not regret it, Tom had assured her. He loved working with his hands and was looking forward to tackling the house repairs. He even asked her permission to replant the garden. Eva had been completely won over by Tom's enthusiasm and eagerness to jump in and get started. She recognized an answer to her prayers when she saw it and quickly agreed to the lease.

"Good morning, Tom," Eva said brightly. "Come on in. Let's sit over here by the window."

Tom followed Eva to a small table situated in front of the floor to ceiling windows that let in the morning sun. The room was very large and had a small table by the east windows and a small sitting area in the corner by the west windows. Outside the other floor to ceiling windows was a large oak tree, perfectly positioned to block the hot, late day sun in the summer. It was a warm and inviting space. "I made us some raspberry iced tea, I hope you like it."

"That sounds delicious, thank you," Tom said as he sat where she indicated. As Eva poured his tea, Tom pulled his computer tablet from his bag and began to show Eva pictures of the work he was doing on her house. They were so engrossed in discussing the renovations that they did not hear Lillian come in.

"Oh, excuse me," Lillian said as she entered the room and noticed Tom sitting at the small table. "I didn't know you had company, Eva."

"Tom Walsh," Tom said as he rose to introduce himself to Lillian.

"It's very nice to meet you Tom," Lillian replied and then looked to Eva who seemed quite happy for a change.

"Not at all, Lillian," Eva said warmly. "Tom was nice enough to bring me pictures of the work he is doing on my house. He really is a Godsend to me."

"Thank you, Eva," Tom said modestly. "It has been my pleasure to do some real work for a change instead of sitting at a desk. Speaking of work"— he turned toward Lillian—"I need to get back to mine. I want to get that roof fixed on the back porch before it rains again. It was nice to meet you, Lillian. Eva, as always, it was a pleasure to see you. Thank you for the tea, it was delicious."

"Come by anytime, Tom," Eva said agreeably, "and thank you again for all your hard work. It does my heart good to know that you are taking care of things for me."

"It's truly my pleasure, Eva. You ladies have a great day and I'll see you soon."

"Here, let me get that for you."

"Great, thanks!" Annie said to the man holding the door for her as she maneuvered through the doorway with her oversized bouquet of flowers.

"Beautiful flowers," Tom added as Annie made her way across the lobby of Magnolia Lane headed to Lillian's room with her weekly delivery.

"Thanks again," she said over her shoulder as she stepped into the waiting elevator. By the time Annie turned to get a look at the man, he was already gone.

"Knock, knock," Annie called out as she entered Lillian's room with the large flower arrangement.

"Oh, Annie, those are amazing!" Lillian exclaimed as she saw the huge bouquet of flowers in Annie's arms. "My goodness, Annie. They are gorgeous! Here, put them down right over here on the table where they can get plenty of morning sun," Eva said as she cleared away the two glasses she and Tom had used just moments before. "You just missed Tom my renter and resident handyman. He's such a nice young man and he's new in town. Single, too."

Before Annie had a chance to respond, Eva added, "He left only a couple of minutes ago, perhaps you saw him in the lobby? He's tall with dark hair and an athletic build. He's such a nice young man, an architect I think he said. He's a college friend of my granddaughter Rachel's husband. A very nice young man, indeed." She smiled at Annie.

"A man did hold the door for me as I came into the lobby," Annie said helpfully. "It could have been him, but I never actually saw him."

"Well, maybe next time," Eva said hopefully as she gathered her things, preparing to head down to the lobby for a rousing game of Bingo with a few of the other residents. "It's always nice to see you, Annie," she said politely as she left the room, adding, "I do so enjoy Lillian's flowers."

"Come sit for a bit." Lillian indicated a chair in the small sitting area she and Eva shared. "Tell me what's new in your life."

"Well," Annie began, "I started a yoga class with Becca on Monday and Thursday mornings at the fitness center downtown. Thursday was my first class and

I'm still a little sore from stretching muscles I didn't know I had, but the best part of the day was lunch and shopping afterward."

"It sounds like you and Becca picked up right where you left off," Lillian said, smiling at Annie. "I'm so glad to see that you are settling in and making Magnolia Creek your home again."

"Thanks, Lillian, I am too," Annie agreed. "Sometimes it's hard for me to believe I've only been here a few months. I feel like this is where I am meant to be. Speaking of 'meant to be,' there's something I'd like to talk to you about."

"Of course, my dear, Lillian said warmly, "I'm all ears."

"I'm thinking of opening a flower shop in Magnolia Creek," she announced proudly. She told Lillian of the incident in the backyard with the watering can, and relayed her conversation with her parents. I have already spoken with my accountant Mr. Duffy regarding the funding"

"Annie, I think it's a wonderful idea! Truly inspired," Lillian exclaimed. Lillian's enthusiastic encouragement was icing on the cake for Annie. She respected her friend's opinion and admired her attitude toward life. "I'm so glad you are supportive of this too! I'm going to speak to Becca when I see her this afternoon so she can help me search for just the right location."

"Speaking of Becca," Annie continued excitedly, circling back to their earlier conversation, "she and Scott have invited me to their house for a BBQ this afternoon. Just a casual family dinner in the backyard, but I'm really looking forward to it. Becca tells me Scott is famous for his ribs, so I'm planning to skip lunch to prepare for the feast! I don't know what I would do without Becca. It's truly a blessing to have such a good friend" Annie said honestly.

Annie caught the shift in Lillian's gaze and intuitively knew she was thinking of Grandma Abby.

"It must be hard for you," Annie said softly to Lillian, "losing someone you knew and loved your whole life."

Lillian smiled and nodded slightly, dabbing at her eyes with the hankie she kept tucked up her sleeve. "It is," she said matter-of-factly, "but at my age I've gotten quite a lot of practice at saying good-bye to family and friends. As much as I miss them, I am comforted to know that I will see them again when the Good Lord calls me home."

Annie witnessed a peace settling over Lillian as she spoke and it gave her comfort as well. Annie decided this would be a good time to leave Lillian to her memories and be on her way.

CHAPTER 16

Now that Annie had talked about her idea with Lillian, she felt a sense of urgency to act. For the first time in her life, Annie knew exactly what she was meant to do.

After speaking with her parents, she had contacted the accountant who had handled the inheritance her grandmother had left her and the financial planner he had recommended she work with. Both had assured her that she would have the necessary funds to open her own business, but they insisted that she submit a business plan. With their help, she began that process with vigor.

As she told Lillian she would, Annie asked Becca to look for the perfect location for the new flower shop. Her childhood friend had been a realtor for several years and was well versed in the properties and shopping patterns in Magnolia Creek, the former due to her profession and the latter due to the fact that she loved to shop. It was a perfect combination and Becca was thrilled at the news that Annie was going into business for herself.

"Are you kidding me?" Becca asked incredulously. "I can't wait to get started. In fact, I think I may already have the ideal location!"

"Seriously?" Annie asked, stunned by Becca's pronouncement.

"Oh my goodness Annie," Becca rattled on, her enthusiasm absolutely palpable, "it's perfect, absolutely perfect. At least I think so, but of course it's up to you, it's your shop. But I just know you'll love it!" Her eyes were bright with excitement.

"What's she going to love?" Scott asked, coming into the kitchen to get the ribs Becca had pulled out of the slow cooker. "And what has you so worked up? Did you sell something?"

"Not exactly," she answered him. "Can I tell him?" she asked Annie quietly.

"Tell me what?" Scott wanted to know. "Just what are you two up to?" he prodded.

"I've decided to open a business," Annie told him matter-of-factly, "and Becca thinks she may already have the perfect location in mind."

"That's my gal," Scott said, kissing his wife on the cheek as he picked up the platter of par-boiled ribs and headed for the back door, "always prepared. You knew she was a Girl Scout, right?"

"Of course she did, genius," Becca teased her husband playfully, "we grew up together, remember? We were Girl Scouts together."

"So, where is it?" Annie asked Becca after Scott went back outside.

"It's actually right on Main Street," Becca told her, "on a corner lot with access to the alley beside and behind for deliveries and extra parking. It used to be a jewelry store, but the property has been tied up in probate since the owner died last year. A broker in my office just listed it a couple of weeks ago and we toured it on our caravan last Wednesday. Annie, I can't wait for you to see it. It has a beautiful façade with large windows for your arrangements, glass display cases in the front area, and a large back room that you could use for a work room. You'd have to put in refrigeration units I suppose, but if I remember correctly there's plenty of room for those in the storage area at the rear of the store."

It sounded absolutely perfect to Annie and she asked Becca to arrange a showing as soon as possible. Now that she had momentum, Annie was going full steam ahead.

Over the next several weeks, Annie managed to make significant progress on turning her dream a reality, but the process was not exactly what she had expected. Having never owned a business before, Annie found it challenging and exciting at the same time. It was hard work and at times she thought the stress would do her in, but in her heart she knew that this was the path she was meant to follow. Annie knew that through her work, many lives would be touched by love and beauty.

....

From the love of flowers her grandmother cultivated in her as a child, her experience in the flower shop all through college, her inheritance of property and capital to fund her dream, the weekly deliveries to Magnolia Lane, down to the availability of what had to be the perfect location for her shop, everything had fallen into place. Not easily, and certainly not without challenges, but neatly in its own way, as if by design.

The architect her accountant found would meet her on Monday morning to do the preliminary walk through and discuss her vision for the shop. His name was Tom, or was it Tim? It didn't matter; he had promised to have the preliminary designs to her by the end of the week and, if they met with her approval, he would review them with the contractor on Monday.

"Wow," she said softly, "things certainly are moving quickly."

A few short months ago, she was just settling into her new home and new life in Magnolia Creek. However, instead of feeling anxiety over the speed at which this project was moving forward, she was actually quite calm. Since the day the idea began to form in her mind, it had just felt right.

CHAPTER 17

Tom Walsh arrived as scheduled to meet Annie Reed at the storefront on Main Street. Her accountant had contacted him through a referral from his friend Paul Wexler to draw up plans for a flower shop Annie was planning to open in town. Tom was happy to take the job for two reasons, the most important being that he really wanted to get to know Annie Reed. Tom loved his work but the woman he had heard so much about intrigued him. Eva had spoken very highly of the young woman who delivered flowers to Magnolia Lane each week. Tom's trips to see Eva generally took place during the week so except for the single occasion he'd had to hold the door for her, he had not yet had the opportunity to formally meet Ms. Reed. He was definitely looking forward to it.

When Tom arrived, Annie caught herself blushing just a bit. Tom was tall and unassuming, not quite handsome, but very comfortable in his own skin. Annie liked that combination.

"Tom Walsh" he said to Annie, reaching out to shake her hand.

"Annie Reed," she said in reply, taking his hand.

"It's nice to finally meet the legend. I hear you have quite a fan club at Magnolia Lane," Tom explained.

Annie looked at him quizzically. "Magnolia Lane? How would you know about?" she began, but he interrupted her quickly and explained that he rented Eva Gordon's house and was a friend of her granddaughter's husband Paul.

"I've heard quite a bit about your generosity with your flowers and your time. Now you're opening your own business," he said with admiration. "I'm impressed."

"Thank you," Annie replied, more than a little flattered that Tom Walsh was impressed with her. "It seemed like the right thing to do."

Eva and Lillian had spoken of Tom several times so, although she had not met him until now, she knew quite a bit about him. It seemed that they had told Tom about her as well. Annie decided that suited her just fine.

Annie and Tom spent the next hour covering every inch of the store in exhaustive detail. Tom asked about her plans for using the large display windows in the front, what were her thoughts on traffic patterns, and did she plan to add any refrigeration cases in the front of the store. They discussed lighting and flooring, countertops, and placement of outlets and switches.

Annie thought she had a clear idea of what she wanted the space to look like, and it was amazing to her how many details Tom was able to extract from her.

He reminded her of one of those police sketch artists she had seen on TV. He asked things in different ways to get different perspectives, and Annie was amazed at the number of details he was able to gather from her mental picture.

There were so many decisions to make that by the time they were finished her head was spinning.

"Have you had lunch?" Tom asked Annie as they were leaving the shop. "They have fabulous fried chicken at the Victorian Café on Thursdays."

"It is good, and it happens to be one of my favorites, but I'd better not," she said, looking toward her car. "I have so much to do today and I promised my attorney I would review the contracts by the end of the day to let him know if I had any questions. That alone could take me hours. It's not exactly my area of expertise."

"Well then, you're in luck," Tom responded brightly, "because it just so happens to be mine." Annie looked at him skeptically and asked how it was that contract law was a specialty of an architect.

"Come on," he urged her playfully, "I'll tell you over lunch."

Tom Walsh did not disappoint her. Not with lunch and certainly not with the contract. He answered each of her questions clearly and in a language she could understand. The fried chicken spoke for itself.

"So I have to know," Annie began, "now that you've regaled me with your legal brilliance, how is it that you know so much about the law? Did you study it in college?"

"Yes, for a time," Tom explained, "but it was my father's dream for me. His expectation for me is probably a more accurate description as he 'expected' me to follow in his footsteps and become a partner in his firm. You know, carry on the family tradition."

"I see," Annie said, "but I take it you had other plans?"

"Well, not at first," Tom explained. "I idolized my father and his approval meant the world to me. But I grew up. I realized that I was not like him, nor would I ever be, and that being myself was never going to be good enough for him. It was a hard lesson, and one I didn't fully learn until my junior year. That's when I told him I was changing my major. It was my passion to build and I wanted to be an architect."

"Ouch," Annie said with concern. "How did that go over?"

"Let's just say he did not take it well," Tom explained, "and he cut off my tuition. My mother intervened and I changed schools. After graduation I moved to L.A. and eventually opened my own firm."

"So, you're a business owner as well," Annie concluded. "What brought you here? I mean, how does a, I'm assuming successful"—Annie teased him—"architect with his own firm in L.A. end up in a small town in southeastern Virginia?"

"Well, why I left L.A. may be a story for another time"—he dodged slightly—"but how I ended up here is easy. Paul Wexler and I were roommates in college when I was pre-law," Tom explained. "I visited here many times with Paul during school breaks and fell in love with the quiet beauty and slower pace of life. Paul introduced me to Eva and"—he concluded with a smile and a wave of his hand—"here I am. But enough about me, Annie Reed, how did you end up a business owner in Magnolia Creek?"

"That," she told him, using his own words against him as she stood up from the table, "is a story for another time."

"It's a date," he responded quickly, pleased at the thought of seeing Annie again socially. Before she could object, he said, "Saturday night? I'll pick you up around seven."

"I can't, Tom, I'm sorry," Annie said, realizing that she really was sorry she couldn't make it. She had promised the ladies she would join them for an entertaining evening of canasta at Magnolia Lane and she was looking forward to hearing their stories about her Grandma Abby's life as a young woman.

"Another time then," he said, trying not to show his disappointment. There was something about Annie that intrigued him. She was definitely different than the type of women he was accustomed to dating in L.A. That was unquestionably in her favor, he mused, thinking about some of the women he had known during his time there. None of which, by the way, could be considered wife material.

Wife? Where on earth had that come from? Tom wondered with alarm. *Who said anything about a wife?*

Its just dinner, he assured himself quickly. *Dinner. Let's just start with dinner.*

Annie watched Tom's expression as it changed quickly with whatever was running through his mind, while she explained why she couldn't make it on Saturday. It was actually comical, she thought, as he shook off his thoughts and responded with an alternate option.

"Well, I certainly can't compete with an offer like that," Tom said, "but how about a compromise? Dinner on Sunday and you can bring your friends with you."

"Tempting," Annie replied slowly, considering Tom's offer. "What do you have in mind? Are you cooking?"

"Absolutely not," he replied a little too quickly. "Not that I couldn't cook you dinner, and I'd like to reserve the option for the near future but I'll leave Sunday dinner to the experts. And by experts I mean Marie and her staff at the café. Have you had her pot roast?" "Not yet," Annie replied, smiling at the look on Tom's face, "but it sounds like I'm missing out."

They agreed that Annie would talk with the ladies on Saturday night and extend Tom's generous, if somewhat transparent, offer.

CHAPTER 18

"So who was that nice looking gentleman you were having lunch with at the café on Monday?" Lillian asked innocently as she dealt the cards for their first game.

"What?" Annie asked, surprised by Lillian's question. "How did you know about that?"

"There are no secrets in a small town like Magnolia Creek, Annie. You should know that by now, dear. Besides, a handsome young man like Tom Walsh is a hot commodity in a town this size. People notice."

"So you already knew who he was, did you? What else do you know?" Annie prodded.

"I know that he seems quite taken with you, Miss Annie Reed. He has been increasing his visits to Eva and commenting on my flowers for weeks now. I suspect he was hoping to get some insight on when you would be coming by so he could 'bump into you' again."

"Well, it turns out he's an architect and I've hired him to design my new shop," Annie explained.

"Well now, isn't that a happy coincidence?" Betty Lou interjected with a knowing smile.

"It certainly is," Winnie agreed, winking pointedly at her friend.

"And just what do you two know about it?" Annie asked as she turned her attention on Winnie and Betty Lou.

"Let's just say that it doesn't hurt to know people," Betty Lou responded with a grin.

"Exactly what does that mean?" Annie asked her, slightly amused at the thought of being set up by her well-meaning friends.

"Don't you worry, Annie. Betty Lou just means that when she heard you were purchasing the old jewelry store, she knew that you would need some help converting it into a flower shop. Eva mentioned that Tom was an architect by trade and, well, one thing led to another, and *voila!* Mr. Duffy recommended Tom for the job," Lillian said, obviously quite pleased with the results of their efforts to bring Annie and Tom together. "He is a very well respected architect, Annie. We did our homework on your Mr. Walsh. We certainly wouldn't have suggested you use someone less qualified."

"Okay, first of all, he's not *my* Mr. Walsh and secondly, why didn't you just tell me? Why go to all the trouble of getting Mr. Duffy to recommend him?"

"Annie, you have so much on your plate at the moment, we didn't want to burden you," Betty Lou explained convincingly. "We know you trust Mr. Duffy and a recommendation from him would seal the deal, so to speak."

"Besides, we didn't want to take a chance that you would think we were trying to fix you up," Winnie said with a knowing nod to her friends. They just rolled their eyes at her obvious attempt to deflect their true motive.

"So that's what this is really about?" Annie asked, unable to hide her amusement at Winnie's failed attempt to deceive her. "You didn't think I had too much on my plate to handle another decision, you just didn't want me to dismiss him instantly because I thought you were meddling in my love life. Which, of course, you are," she added with a stern look at the three of them.

"So how *was* your lunch, dear?" Lillian asked innocently, trying to turn the conversation back to Annie and Tom.

"Okay, I give up," Annie conceded gracefully, obviously outmaneuvered by the three old ladies. "It was actually very nice. Did you know Tom studied to be a lawyer before deciding to become an architect?" The ladies had not known that but were intrigued. "His father is a lawyer in San Francisco," Annie continued, certain that Tom would not mind her discussing details of his life that he had openly shared with her during their lunch together. "He was actually very helpful in translating the contracts for the shop into layman's terms so I could get them signed and returned to my attorney.

"Speaking of dining with Tom," Annie began, noticing she had their full attention, "he's invited us all to Sunday dinner at the Victorian café tomorrow."

"All of us?" Betty Lou asked, a bit skeptical that Tom would want to share his time with Annie with the three of them.

"All of us," Annie assured her. "He knows how important you all are to me and if he is, as you suggest, trying to find opportunities to spend time with me, then it's rather astute of him to engage three willing coconspirators, don't you think?"

"Oh, he's good," Winnie said agreeably, "because who in their right mind would turn down pot roast at the café? Not me, that's for sure."

Lillian laughed at Winnie's enthusiasm for quality pot roast and said, "I think it's a wonderful idea, but let's see if we can get Mr. Walsh to join us for Sunday morning services first." They all agreed that Annie would invite Tom to meet them at church for the late service the next morning and they would all go to the café afterward.

Tom readily agreed when Annie called him and told him of the ladies' invitation to church. He promised to make reservations for the five of them and told her he would see them in the morning.

Tom arrived at the church after Annie and the ladies were already seated. He found them and sat down beside Annie just before the first hymn began. "Good morning," he whispered to the ladies as they rose to sing.

"Good morning, Mr. Walsh," they greeted him pleasantly. "We're glad you could join us."

To Annie's surprise, Tom seemed quite familiar with the hymns and customs of the traditional church service she and the ladies preferred. She would have to be sure to ask him about that since the church had become an integral part of her life in Magnolia Creek. Then she wondered why she hadn't seen him there before. Perhaps he attended a different church, or, much like herself, had not attended regularly until she was invited.

It turned out that Annie didn't need to ask Tom about his churchgoing habits. After all, they were in the company of three "little old ladies," as they liked to refer to themselves when it suited them, and they didn't waste a second after they were seated at their table in the café before the questioning began. "So tell us Tom, were you raised in the church?"

"I was," Tom replied, looking first to Lillian and then to the other women at the table. "My sister and I have attended church regularly with my parents since we were children. In fact, I was an altar boy."

"You don't say," Betty Lou piped in, smiling broadly, obviously taken with Tom. "So why haven't we seen you in church before today?"

Tom took the questioning in stride, knowing the ladies were not only curious but, more importantly, they were looking out for the welfare of their "adopted granddaughter" Annie. If Tom had any intentions toward Annie, and he was quite sure he did, then he would have to pass muster with these fine ladies.

"Honestly," he explained, "I just hadn't gotten around to it yet. I know that's a lame excuse, but it's the truth. Since I came to Magnolia Creek, I have been focused on the work I brought with me for my clients in L.A., and in my spare time I have been working on Eva's house to get it back in shape while the weather is being cooperative. Yours was the first invitation I've received and it was a welcome one at that. I like the church. The service was right on point and the congregation was very welcoming. I'll definitely be back." They all agreed that it would be wonderful to have Tom become part of their church family and the matter was settled to everyone's satisfaction.

CHAPTER 19

Annie and Tom saw quite a bit of each other socially and professionally over the next month. Plans for the shop were final and the construction was well underway. Tom had been very helpful in finding good quality workmen to make the necessary updates to the old building. With his business dealings in L.A. winding down, he had the time to dedicate to overseeing the work personally. Besides, he reasoned with himself, it afforded him more time to spend with Annie when she popped in to check on their progress.

"So how's my future looking today?" Annie asked Tom as she came in through the back door of the shop carrying a file box from her home office.

"Here, let me take that," Tom said, jumping up from his seat at the counter where he was reviewing invoices.

"It needs to go in the safe," Annie said as Tom took the heavy box from her. "The safe is ready to use, right?" she confirmed as Tom headed toward the large jewelers' safe that had come with the building.

"Absolutely," he assured her, "and there's lots of room. Maybe even enough to store your entire shoe collection." He joked. "Well, maybe not all of them but at least your favorites."

"Very funny" Annie laughed. She knew she owned a lot of shoes, but it was just part of who she was and she didn't mind Tom's joke at her expense. After all, he was absolutely right. The truth was she loved the easy way she and Tom joked with each other. Besides, she knew Tom's weakness was tools. Hand tools, power tools, small tools, and big tools, he loved them all. He enjoyed building new things and fixing whatever broke. She could see how happy this job made him, handling things for her while she took care of her flowers and deliveries. It felt right to have him be a part of her life.

"So have you thought any more about this weekend?" Tom asked as Annie settled in beside him at the counter.

"Actually I have," Annie replied, "and I'd love to go to the beach. I don't know if I'm up for swimming, but the thought of a nice dinner with an ocean view and a walk on the beach afterward sounds amazing. I could really use a break. I feel like I've been going nonstop for weeks."

"You have been," Tom said with concern in his voice. "That's why I thought a whole day away would do you good."

Tom had arranged to have lunch delivered to the shop so they could spend a little time together before she was off on her afternoon errands. They discussed their plans while they ate. "We can leave early in the morning and drop off your deliveries to Magnolia Lane on the way out of town," Tom suggested. "We can grab a late breakfast on the way and take the scenic route along the James River. If you're not in a hurry to get to the coast, we could stop at Yorktown on the way and tour the historic settlement there. I know you love history and very few places have more history than Virginia."

"That all sounds perfect," Annie agreed. "I haven't been to Yorktown since my last field trip with Becca in the third grade. It was the year I moved away."

"Then it's settled. I'll pick you up Saturday morning at eight," Tom said as he began to clear away their sandwich wrappers and prepared to get back to work.

"It's a date," Annie said, kissing him lightly on the lips as she turned to leave.

"Not so fast, boss lady," Tom said, grabbing her around the waist and pulling her close. "That's not nearly enough to keep me going until Saturday." He kissed her passionately, holding her to him until he heard the voices of the workers carrying through the doorway as they returned from their lunch break.

"Well, okay then." Annie was clearly thrown off balance by Tom's lingering kiss. "I um, need to get going," she said as she attempted to compose herself before the workers stepped into the shop.

Tom watched her leave without looking back at him, pleased with himself for clearly giving Annie a moment to remember as she returned to her daily routine.

....

"That man is dangerous," Annie told Becca later that afternoon as they worked on the flowers for her Saturday delivery to Magnolia Lane.

"What do you mean?" Becca asked her friend. "Dangerous how?"

"Dangerous as in making my palms sweat," Annie said emphatically, "that's how!"

"Well," Becca commented with delight, "that sounds like a very enjoyable kind of dangerous to me."

"Oh, it's enjoyable all right," Annie agreed. "Wow."

Becca had been spending more and more time working with Annie in the barn lately, as she continued her deliveries to Magnolia Lane. It had started out as a helping hand when Annie had taken on a paying job from Marie, supplying flowers to the Victorian Café each week. She had a weekly delivery of a large bouquet for the front entrance, and smaller bud vases for each of the tables. When Marie had a special occasion—such as a wedding rehearsal dinner, a birthday, or anniversary— she would ask Annie for special centerpieces that the guests could take home with them as a memento of their evening.

It was a lucrative deal as the café was a very popular destination for special occasions. More importantly, it provided Annie with enough income to keep her special deliveries going at Magnolia Lane. Annie knew she brought a lot of joy to residents and staff alike. And the joy it brought her was just icing on the cake as far as she was concerned. She couldn't imagine a time when she wouldn't be doing this work.

"Have you thought about asking for volunteers from church to help with your deliveries?" Becca asked. "I'll bet you could get any number of ladies, or even men to help you out."

"Don't get me wrong," Becca said quickly as she saw Annie's expression of concern, "I love helping you. It's just that when your shop opens, you're going to be even busier than you are now and I won't always be available to help. With Scott and the kids and my blooming real estate career, no pun intended"—Becca smiled—"it might be a good idea to enlist more troops. The women could organize and assemble the bouquets, with some basic training from you of course, and the men could help with the supplies and deliveries. It really would be a wonderful gift to share with them, Annie. I see how much joy this work brings you. Just think of how many other people you could bless in the same way."

"You're right," Annie agreed with Becca "and I will definitely give it serious consideration. After my date with Tom," Annie clarified. "Quite frankly," she confided in Becca, "I can't seem to think of anything else at the moment."

They laughed together over Annie's admission and went back to discussing Tom's numerous good qualities, not the least of which was that he was a terrific kisser.

....

CHAPTER 20

Annie loved taking walks around her property with Daisy. Especially now, when life seemed so hectic, it was her perfect escape. She would wander through the woods, visit the little prayer garden she found on her first day, and play fetch with Daisy in the backyard.

It's so peaceful here, she thought to herself, and it really has become my home. It felt good to be in a place with so many wonderful memories, and yet she was not living in the past. In fact, she was living a life that she had literally never even dreamed of. And she loved it. She loved her home, her friends, her work, and she loved Tom. I love him, she thought to herself.

"I do love him," Annie said aloud, unsure of how she felt about this admission. "I love Tom Walsh."

Daisy had returned the ball and barked once when Annie made no move to pick it up. Still lost in thought about how it felt to realize she was in love, Annie picked up the ball and threw it as hard as she could, shouting, "I love Tom Walsh!" She actually felt like a schoolgirl again with her first crush. She realized that she couldn't stop smiling and quickly gave up trying. She was happy. Truly happy.

"C'mon, Daisy, let's take a walk," she called as she headed into the woods. She suddenly had energy to burn and felt like exploring. Daisy kept pace with Annie, all the while diving in and out of the underbrush looking for animals to chase. She would weave in and out of the trees looking back frequently to make sure Annie was still there.

As she approached the small rise, Annie noticed a large oak tree with a swing hanging from one of the sturdy lower branches. It swayed slightly in the breeze that blew through the smaller trees surrounding the clearing. She could hear a faint creaking as the wooden seat twisted the old heavy chains in the wind.

Annie was completely mesmerized by the sight and sound of this stately oak tree in a serene clearing in the middle of what appeared to be an overgrown thicket. In fact, if she had not been looking in that direction when she passed by, she may have missed it completely.

How many times had she walked by this hidden treasure without knowing it was there and why had her mother never mentioned it? The tree looked like it must be at least one hundred years old so she must have know about it and had probably even played on the swing. Yet she had never mentioned it to Annie. Come to think of it, neither had Grandma. All those weekends and summers she spent at her grandma's and not once did any of them mention the tree swing. She found that very odd.

As she began to make her way into the clearing to get a better look, she heard Daisy begin to bark frantically then suddenly stop. Almost immediately, she heard a loud yelp and thrashing in the brush. Now completely focused on Daisy making her way loudly through the underbrush, all thoughts of the tree swing were gone.

As Daisy burst into view, the smell of the skunk she'd apparently just tangled with preceded her. Annie knew she was in for it when Daisy came at her without slowing down. "Oh no you don't," Annie exclaimed loudly, sidestepping Daisy at the last second to avoid being knocked to the ground.

"Stop! Sit!" she commanded loudly. Daisy skidded slightly on the wet ground as she turned to make another pass, stopping just short of Annie's feet. She whimpered miserably as she rubbed her paws over her eyes to wipe off the skunk spray. It was a useless gesture as she had taken the brunt of the attack to her face and the rubbing just transferred the offensive spray to her paws and front legs.

"Oh, Daisy, you poor thing," Annie spoke softly to her, covering her own nose and mouth as best she could. "Lets get you home and into the washtub. I'm afraid you'll be sleeping on the porch tonight, my friend. There's no way you're coming into the house smelling like that!"

"How do I get rid of skunk spray?" Annie asked, as soon as Winnie picked up the phone.

"You or Daisy?" she asked Annie, not missing a beat.

"Thankfully, it's Daisy," Annie replied, "but I'm pretty sure at least some of it will end up on me before this ordeal is over."

"Quite right," Winnie said, getting down to business. "You should find an old washtub, one of those big metal ones with handles, hanging in the barn. I think Abby kept it just inside the door on the left. Bring that out to the side yard by the driveway so you can tie Daisy to the porch. Then put on a pair of Ben's old coveralls and try to get as much of the skunk smell as you can off her. The only thing that will work is," pausing mid-sentence, Winnie asked, "Do you have a pencil? You'll need to write this down."

"I'm ready," Annie assured her friend, smiling at Winnie's take-charge attitude.

"Okay, start with a quart of hydrogen peroxide. Abby usually kept that under the bathroom sink," she offered helpfully, "1/4 cup of baking soda and just a couple of teaspoons of dish soap. The liquid kind, not the powder for the dishwasher. That wouldn't be too good for poor Daisy."

"Got it" Annie smiled at the last part of the instructions. "Well, I'd better get to it," Annie said, trying to wrap up her conversation with Winnie, "thanks so much for the advice. I don't know what I would have done if you hadn't been home to take my call."

"I'm happy to help, kiddo. Now don't forget to get a pair of your grandpa's old coveralls from the cabinet in the barn. And gloves," she added quickly, "don't forget the gloves! The rubber ones work best. You definitely do not want to smell skunk every time you bring your fork to your mouth for the next week or so." Winnie laughed. "No, ma'am, that would not be good. I can't believe I almost forgot about the gloves," she mused as Annie anxiously awaited her opportunity to get off the phone and tend to Daisy.

"I must be getting old," she said with finality. "Yep," she continued, oblivious to Annie's desire to end the call quickly, "nothing I can do about that I suppose. I just pray the good Lord calls me home before I forget my own name."

"Well," Annie interjected quickly as Winnie's thought took her away, "I pray that day is a long way off, Winnie. And thanks again. I'd better run and get Daisy into the tub before that smell sets in any further. I'll call you in a couple of days when it's safe to come over and maybe we can have some lunch out on the porch if the weather's nice."

"Of course, of course, you go take care of that sweet dog of yours and I'll look forward to hearing from you when the coast is clear." They said their good-byes and Annie set off to collect what she needed to de-skunk poor Daisy.

CHAPTER 21

Saturday morning started out a bit foggy, but by the time they had dropped off the flowers at Magnolia Lane and headed toward Richmond, the skies had begun to clear and the sun was already beginning to warm the air. Tom had arrived promptly at eight o'clock and had helped Annie load the truck. They had gotten permission from the manager of Magnolia Lane for Annie to leave her truck parked in the lot for the day so Tom could take his car to the beach. He wanted the option of putting the top down if the weather permitted and it certainly looked promising for the afternoon.

By all accounts, it was a perfect day. They had stopped for breakfast at a place Tom had heard about from the workers that lived in Richmond. It was southern cooking at its finest and they spent a good portion of their meal discussing grits. Neither of them was accustomed to eating grits and while Annie's grandfather had loved them, no one else in her family shared his enthusiasm. They watched other diners with wonder as they ordered them with butter or cheese or as one diner requested, syrup and gravy. They laughed about that for quite awhile as they began their scenic drive along the James River.

The drive was beautiful, just as Annie suspected it would be. The road wound along the river and passed historic plantations. They passed through tiny towns with rich history and after about twenty minutes of driving, Annie completely gave up on counting the historical markers that lined the roadways. "So much history," Annie mused aloud. "During both the Revolutionary War and the Civil War, this river was a major thoroughfare for troops and supplies. There were hundreds of battles fought along its banks."

She and Tom discussed their love of history as they traveled along the river, finding even more common ground between them as they drove.

Annie found it very comfortable being with Tom. Had Tom known what she was thinking, he would have agreed with her completely.

The couple arrived early enough to put the top down and drive along the coast roads enjoying the sun and ocean breezes. They decided to save the stop at Yorktown for another day and focus on the relaxing waves of the ocean and the warm sun that seemed to burn off all worries and cares. They spent the afternoon walking in the sand and surf and wandering around the small shops that lined the area near the beach. They enjoyed a wonderful dinner at a local restaurant dining on fresh seafood at a candlelit table overlooking the sea.

When dinner was over, they lingered over their coffee, watching the sun set on their relaxing day at the beach.

"We'd better head back." Tom sighed as they held hands on the way to the car.

"I know," Annie said softly, "but I just hate for this day to end.

"Thank you, Tom," Annie said tenderly, turning into him as he reached to open her door. "I can't remember when I've had such a wonderful time."

Tom took Annie's face in his hands and kissed her long and hard. "I'm crazy about you, Annie Reed," he said as he stood back to allow them both to catch their breath. "You are beautiful, smart and funny, and I'm falling in love with you."

Annie had never heard more welcoming words. She kissed Tom repeatedly, hugging him close with no intention of ever letting him go.

"So, can I take it that you feel the same way about me?" he asked her as she hugged him tightly.

"Oh, Tom," she said, "I had no idea how much those words meant to me until I heard you say them. I didn't dare to let myself think about where this relationship was headed. It all seems to have happened so fast, and yet it feels like we belong together. Am I crazy?"

"You're not crazy," Tom assured her with a grin, "at least not about that."

"I think I knew you were dangerous the day you pulled up in front of my shop in this sexy sports car and spoke my name," Annie confided. "Since that day I have come to appreciate what a truly remarkable man you are, Tom Walsh. You are loving and considerate, generous and kind. You make me laugh and make me think about life in new ways. I felt anxiety about letting you into my life and real fear about letting you anywhere near my heart, but now I realize that I had no choice in the matter, you are already there. I love you, Tom, and there's nothing you can do about it." Her smile widened as she saw the joy and relief on Tom's face.

"Whoo-hoo!" Tom yelled out loud, drawing attention from several patrons in the parking lot. "She loves me!" he yelled even louder, attracting stares and applause from several of the couples nearby. He picked Annie up and swung her around, kissing her enthusiastically before putting her down again. Annie laughed out loud at Tom's excitement and quickly slid into the car as he opened her door.

"I'm so happy Tom," Annie began after Tom maneuvered the car onto the highway to head back to Magnolia Creek. "It hardly seems possible after the way my last relationship ended. I was so sure I was in love with Jarrod. Maybe I was on some level, but it turned out that he just wasn't the man I thought he was. His betrayal broke my heart. I was so afraid of getting hurt again that I spent three long years avoiding relationships, terrified of letting myself fall for anyone again. I just don't think I can go through that kind of heartbreak again."

Tom reached over and took Annie's hand in his, entwining their fingers as he spoke. "I'm sorry you had to go through that, Annie. Getting your heart broken is the worst kind of pain and I promise you that the last thing I would ever want to do is to make you feel that way again."

Annie looked at Tom and saw the conviction on his face, illuminated by the dashboard lights as he focused on the road ahead. She squeezed his hand, and relaxed back in her seat as she said, "I believe you."

Tom knew he should tell Annie about Maggie right now while they were talking about past loves, but he could not bring himself to do it. It seemed like a lifetime ago, and they had been so young. He realized that he wasn't ready to think about that part of his life, much less talk about it with Annie, at least not tonight. He loved her, he knew that for certain, and he wanted to enjoy this night, not complicate it. He would find the right time to tell the woman he loved that he had been married before, but it would not be tonight.

"I think it's only fair that I warn you about my family," Tom said a short time later, breaking the comfortable silence. "My parents aren't exactly normal. At least not what I suspect is your version of normal," he said as he smiled in her direction. "As you know, my dad is an attorney. He is happiest when he is working and making money. My mother, on the other hand, is a pillar in the charity community and is happiest when she is raising money for the less fortunate. It's a match made in heaven for them. Dad has a lot of contacts, and Mom knows how to use them to pull off a successful fundraiser. Don't get me wrong," he said candidly, "they aren't horrible people, but they aren't going to win any awards for Parents of the Year."

"Was it really that bad growing up rich?" she chided him amicably.

"It was wonderful actually, but it just wasn't a creative and supportive environment. My parents care too much about appearances and recognition for my taste," he explained. "I prefer to keep a lower profile."

"Oh, your parents are just going to love me then," she said teasingly, "a small town girl who delivers flowers for a living. I can see it now…"

"They are going to love you Annie. Trust me on this. I just have to find the right time to break the news that I am not going to marry the daughter of one of Dad's country club buddies. Believe me, I've dated enough debutantes to know that is never going to happen."

"Exactly how many debs did it take before you figured that out?" Annie asked him in mock indignation.

Tom turned to look at her in the dim light and Annie quickly said with humor in her voice, "No, no, don't tell me! There are some things about you I just don't need to know—and that is definitely one of them."

Tom smiled back at Annie, not saying a word. All in due time, Tom thought to himself. All in due time.

CHAPTER 22

"There you are, Tom!" Betty Lou said, approaching their pew at the church Sunday morning with a woman and young boy in tow. "There's someone I'd like you to meet. Tom, this is Ryan. He and his mother just moved here from Philadelphia."

"It's a pleasure to meet you," Tom said to Ryan, reaching out to shake his hand. "You have a very firm grip. I like that in a man. It shows character."

Ryan smiled broadly at the compliment and seemed to stand just a little taller as he shook Tom's hand.

"Ryan, this is Tom," Betty Lou continued, "and he just moved here a couple of months ago from Los Angeles."

"Do you like baseball?" Ryan asked Tom, not really listening to Betty Lou.

"Like it?" Tom said earnestly. "I love it! In fact, I was just telling Annie here that what this church needs is a baseball team." Tom looked at Annie for support and she nodded agreement, playing along but not sure where Tom was headed. "Is that something you'd like to help me with, Ryan? You know, talk to some of the other guys about getting a team together?"

"Sure." Ryan nodded enthusiastically and turned to his mother. "Can I?"

"Of course," Susannah replied, smiling at Tom. "It would be great for him to meet kids his own age before school starts. Thank you."

"My pleasure Mrs…" Tom raised his eyebrows questioningly as he reached out his hand in introduction, not sure how to address Ryan's mother since Betty Lou had been called away before the introductions were completed.

"Susannah," she replied quickly, reaching out to shake his hand. "Susannah Davidson."

"Nice to meet you, Susannah. This is Annie," Tom said as Annie stepped forward to meet Susannah and Ryan.

"It's a pleasure to meet you both," she said cordially, "and welcome to Magnolia Creek. I have to admit I have only been here a few months myself, but this is my second time around." She smiled at Susannah's quizzical look. "I sort of grew up here. My family moved away when I was about Ryan's age and I just recently returned to put down roots of my own."

Annie and Susannah chatted for a few minutes about the local area and where to find the best shopping, as Tom introduced Ryan to the few kids he already knew. By the time the service started, Tom and Ryan had enlisted three other boys in their brand new baseball team. Even the pastor had gotten in the spirit by offering to recruit the women's group to raise funds to buy matching shirts. It was incredible to Tom how quickly his spur-of-the-moment suggestion had become a reality. He had to admit that he was quite excited himself about getting involved with the kids.

Tom had always wanted to be a dad. Not just a father, but a dad who made time for his kids. He wanted to play catch with his son, have tea parties with his daughter, and provide for his own family. He had never felt especially comfortable with the country club lifestyle his own parents preferred. As he had told Annie on the way home from their date at the beach, he had no interest in high-society life. Tom craved normalcy, a slower pace. He had no interest in keeping up with the Joneses and preferred a sports car to a town car.

He supposed that's what had drawn him to Maggie all those years ago. They shared the vision of a simple and carefree life, away from the pressures and demands of the rich and dying-to-be-famous crowd they had both been raised with.

She was so beautiful, he thought, remembering her soft blond hair, bleached by the California sun, and her tanned and freckled skin, so soft to the touch. He had never met someone so carefree and open, Tom remembered with fondness. The girls he had dated up to that point had all been raised in boarding schools and had been groomed to be society wives, the perfect companions to their very successful husbands. Maggie was a breath of fresh air in his stuffy, buttoned-down world. And she was the reason he decided to leave law school and follow his dreams.

They married in the summer with not one family member present. Just their friends, standing on the beach, listening to them promise to love each other for the rest of their lives, support each other through the good times and the bad, until death do they part. It was a beautiful ceremony, and they meant every word of their vows.

Their marriage lasted three months. When the summer ended, reality set in, and they realized that their vision of a carefree life with no expectations on them was not all they hoped it would be. They divorced amicably, but Tom never saw Maggie again.

I wonder what made me think of her after all these years, he wondered to himself. Maybe just thinking about having a son, he decided. Perhaps he was also thinking about his life with Annie and his hope to one day be the dad he dreamed he'd be.

CHAPTER 23

Annie was not about to let something as simple as a computer problem get in the way of her grand opening. She had worked too hard to make this dream a reality. She just needed to think for a minute and not panic. Who did she know that knew anything about computers? Becca was about as savvy as Annie in that area and Scott was no better. *So,* she thought shrewdly, *who did they call for help?*

"Hey Annie!" Becca answered her cell phone cheerfully. "I thought you'd be busy with the grand opening plans."

"I was," Annie replied, struggling to keep her voice calm, "but I ran into a bit of trouble."

"What kind of trouble," Becca asked, her concern rising. "It's just a computer glitch," Annie explained, "but the revisions I made to the newspaper ads are on my computer and I didn't have a chance to back it up before it choked and died."

"What do you mean 'choked and died,'" Becca asked anxiously, immediately followed by, "never mind, forget I asked. I wouldn't know what you're talking about anyway."

Annie smiled into the phone. Becca's candor was one of the things Annie loved most about her friend, with her sense of humor running a close second. There were no problems with Becca; she said what she meant and did what she said she would do. "Thanks for that," Annie told her friend, actually laughing for the first time since this whole incident started. "I needed a laugh."

"Hang on a minute, Annie, I'll check with Scott—he knows a guy."

A few moments later Scott came on the phone. "Hey, Annie, I hear you're having technical difficulties."

"You could say that," Annie replied, trying not to sound as desperate as she felt. "Becca said you might know a guy who could help?"

"Well," Scott hedged, "yes and no."

Annie waited impatiently for Scott to continue, but he didn't. "Yes and no?" Annie asked in bewilderment. "What does that even mean? I'm kind of in a bind here Scott."

"Okay, okay, calm down, Annie, I'm just having a little fun with you. It's not often I see you flustered and I just couldn't resist. Besides," Scott continued, "he's more of a kid than a guy. He doesn't even drive yet, but he's a whiz at computers and he works cheap. I think he's saving for a car he can't even drive."

"I don't care if he's not potty trained," Annie responded, playing into Scott's teasing, "I need help and I need it now."

"Becca!" Scott called to his wife. "Will you grab me that note on the fridge that looks like a one hundred dollar bill? It has Chad's number on it. Yep, that's the one. Okay, here it is, do you have a pen?"

"Ready," Annie replied, relieved that Scott was able to help and anxious to call his "guy."

As Annie jotted down Chad's number, Becca came back on the line. "Scott says not to introduce him to any pretty girls while he's over there. He's convinced that once Chad discovers girls, he'll be lost to us forever."

"Not to worry," Annie assured her. "I promise to lock him in the back room until he's done." Annie hung up and immediately dialed the number Scott had given her.

"Chad," she began when he answered, "this is Annie Reed."

"I know," Chad replied into his Bluetooth, pausing for effect. "Caller ID."

"I got your number from Scott Jameson," Annie continued. "He recommended I call you to see if you could help me with a computer problem I'm having."

"Sure," Chad replied, suddenly all business. "When do you want me to come over?"

"Would now be too soon for you?" she asked hopefully. "I'm kind of in a bind."

"Now is great," he answered. "What's the address?"

"I'm at Blooms on Main Street, across from the square downtown."

"Okay," he said casually, "I'll be there in about ten minutes."

"The shop's not actually open yet," Annie advised him, "so you'll have to knock and I'll come let you in."

Chad assured her that it was no problem and that he was on his way. She was confident this would all be behind her soon and she would be able to focus on the next crisis.

"Wait!" she exclaimed just before Chad hung up. "Don't you want to know what its doing?"

"No, that's okay," he explained. "Even if you told me, it probably isn't the real problem. Not that you're stupid or anything, it's just that most grownups don't really know much about hardware so it's easier if I see it for myself. It'll just save time that way."

"Okay," Annie said cheerfully, "you're the geek." She smiled to herself and added, "Remember to knock real loud so I can hear it in the back," before she hung up.

Chad was true to his word, and his GPS, knocking on her door ten minutes later. She let him inside, noting that he looked familiar. He was a little taller than her five-foot seven inches with sandy hair that hung in his eyes. His jeans were baggy, but not falling down to show his boxers for all to see. *Thank heavens that fad has passed*, Annie thought.

"So where is your computer?" Chad asked, his eyes roaming around the shop.

"It's in the back office," Annie said as Chad followed her to the rear of the shop.

"You work at the Victorian Café," Annie said over her shoulder as she realized why he looked familiar. "Marie is your mother?"

"Yep," he answered automatically as he sat down at her desk and turned his attention to her computer. Two hours and sixty dollars later, Annie was up and running again. Chad had even created a network for her so when she was using her personal computer she could log into the shared network drive and access work files from anywhere. She was so happy with his work, she sent Chad home with a beautiful arrangement of fresh flowers for his mother. Annie thanked him again as he left with the flowers, telling him to be sure to send his mom over on opening day.

"That was fast," Becca said as she answered Annie's call. "Did Chad get it fixed?"

"All fixed and then some," Annie replied happily. "Please thank Scott for me, would you? He's a real lifesaver."

"Of course," Becca said cheerfully, "but if you don't mind, I'll leave out the part about his heroics. It'll just go to his head and there will be no living with him!"

The women laughed at Becca's description of Scott, mostly because it was true.

CHAPTER 24

The call came in around 2:00 a.m. that the shop had been burglarized. Annie was not accustomed to receiving phone calls in the middle of the night and was a bit confused when the ringing woke her. As she realized it was the phone, a sense of dread crept in, fearing that something bad had happened to one of the ladies.

"Hello, this is Annie Reed," she said quickly into the phone as she answered.

"Annie, this is Sheriff Dodd. I'm sorry to wake you, but there's been a break-in at your shop and I would appreciate it if you could come down here and take a look and tell us if anything is missing."

"Of course," Annie replied, relieved that it wasn't about her friends. "I'll be there in twenty minutes." Memories of the incident at her apartment in Seattle came to mind suddenly, but she dismissed them immediately. This was different. This was not her home and she was no longer alone. She quickly called Tom.

"I'm sorry to wake you, Tom, but I need you," Annie began.

"What happened?" Tom asked, concern in his voice.

"First let me assure you that everyone is okay," she continued. "I just got a call from Sheriff Dodd that there has been a break-in at the shop. He wants me to come down there to see if anything is missing. I would really appreciate it if you were there with me, Tom. I really don't want to do this alone. And I have no idea what kind of damage was done, but I'm sure that it will take some effort to secure the place."

"Of course," he said, already thinking about what he would need to take. "I'll grab my tools and meet you there in twenty minutes. And Annie"—Tom paused—"I love you. We'll get through this together."

"I know we will, Tom. I love you, too," Annie said as she hung up the phone, apprehensive about what she would find at the shop, relieved that everyone she loved was okay, and grateful that Tom would be there with her.

When Annie arrived at the shop, Tom was already there, talking with Sheriff Dodd. "I was just telling Tom here that it looks like kids broke in just to vandalize the place, teenagers by the looks of it."

As Annie and Tom went inside to look around, they noticed that the front windows were intact and the cabinet housing the safe was untouched. They hadn't even bothered with the cash register, which meant they probably knew the shop wasn't open, yet. A few of the glass cases had been smashed, but the refrigeration units were intact. Tom unplugged them so the motors wouldn't burn up and then continued his sweep of the shop. There were a few holes in the drywall, but the majority of the damage was cosmetic or could be fixed with replacement glass.

"Anything missing?" Sheriff Dodd asked as he stepped through the front door, his radio squawking on his shoulder.

"Nothing that we can see" Tom replied, taking another glance around.

"We may have caught a break" the sheriff continued, listening to his radio. "Deputy Marsh pulled over a car full of teens for speeding and driving erratically a few miles outside of town. Seems the driver had been drinking and a search of the vehicle turned up hammers, crowbars, and spray paint. One of the kids started spilling his guts about how the kid driving had forced them to break into a store downtown. He then stole a car for their little joyride. We're bringing the boys in for questioning now."

"Thanks, sheriff, and please keep us posted. In the meantime, I'd like to secure the place to avoid any further damage or theft. Is it all right with you if I get started?" Tom asked respectfully.

"Understood, Tom, just give my techs an hour or so to finish their work and then it's all yours." The sheriff shook hands with both Tom and Annie and headed back to the station.

"How about a hot cup of coffee?" Tom offered. "I put the coffee maker on before I left the house." Annie nodded her agreement and Tom said, "I'll let the techs know we'll be back shortly."

Ten minutes later, Annie sat at Tom's kitchen table holding her mug of hot coffee. "Why would anyone do this?" she asked Tom, bewildered by the whole situation.

"I don't know for sure, Annie," Tom said has he took a seat across from her, "but if it was the teenagers we heard about, maybe they just got caught up in the moment. Boys that age can have a lot of aggression and anger that builds up over small things that most adults have learned to let go of. Not all kids have good role models in their lives or parents who care enough about them to know where they are and what they're doing. It also sounds like maybe some of the kids found themselves in a situation they were unprepared to deal with where the older boy was calling the shots.

"I'm so disappointed about the mess and the work that will need to be done to get ready for the opening," Annie admitted, "but I know it could have been so much worse. Putting it in perspective, I am just so relieved that the call was not about someone we love."

"Just one of your many charms," Tom said, smiling and taking Annie's hands in his.

"What is?" Annie asked him.

"Your unwavering ability to see the positive side of a situation. I love that about you, Annie. You're like a ray of sunshine," he added with a grin.

When they arrived back at the shop, the techs were just finishing up and indicated that Tom could start his work to secure the back door where the teens had entered from the alley.

....

"Annie?" Marie called loudly as she rounded the back of the house. "Are you back here? I knocked, but didn't get an answer."

"I'm back here," Annie replied, "in the garden."

"Hi, Annie," Marie said as she approached Annie sitting cross-legged at the edge of one of her many flowerbeds, where from the looks of it she was taking out a healthy dose of frustration on some unsuspecting weeds. Based on the size of the piles she was building and the sweat on her brow, it appeared that Annie had been at this attack for several hours already this morning.

"Marie," Annie said, surprised to see the café owner in her backyard, especially during the lunch rush. *What on earth could have brought her here?* Annie wondered as she stood to greet her guest.

"Oh please don't get up on my account, Annie. I'm so sorry to disturb you, but I just had to come in person to tell you how sorry I am."

"Sorry?" Annie asked in bewilderment. She motioned for Marie to join her on the back porch.

As she wiped her hands and took a seat on the top step, Annie asked Marie, "What on earth do you mean? What do you have to be sorry for?"

As she sat down next to her, Marie explained about the call she received early this morning to come to the jail to pick up her son Chad. He had been in the car that was pulled over by Deputy Marsh after the break-in at Annie's shop. Annie's reaction went from shock to disappointment to determination as Marie's story unfolded.

Marie told Annie about Chad's absentee father and how he had been in trouble when they lived in Baltimore. "But he had really turned around since moving to Magnolia Creek," she assured Annie, "or at least I thought he had. He was really into computers and cars and all indications of trouble were nonexistent. That's why I was so shocked to get the call this morning, only to learn of Chad's involvement in the break-in."

"Apparently the oldest of the boys, the ringleader it turns out, had actually stolen the car while the other boys were inside the shop," Marie explained to Annie, relaying what the deputy had told her when she went to the station. "So at least there won't be any felony charges to deal with. Most likely Chad will get community service from the judge and enough chores from me to keep him busy from sun up to sun down. I plan to make sure that boy has no time or energy for trouble. You can count on that!"

"If the judge will allow it," Annie proposed, "I'd like Chad to work off his community service at the shop. Not only will it give him the opportunity to make restitution for some of the damage he and his friends had done, but, even more importantly,"—Annie smiled conspiratorially at Marie—"it will give him the opportunity to build a healthy relationship with Tom. If you agree, I'll talk to Tom about it tonight." Marie agreed quickly, grateful for the opportunity for Chad to clean up his own mess. But Annie had much higher expectations of this arrangement. If Tom agreed, and she was certain he would, Annie was convinced that Chad would learn about much more than just cleaning up his own mess working alongside Tom. Chad needed a solid male influence in his life and she was certain that spending quality time with Tom would help the teen regain his positive direction and learn how to avoid getting mixed up with kids who would lead him down the wrong path.

CHAPTER 25

The Grand Opening of Blooms turned out to be everything Annie had hoped for. Tom and Chad had finished the repairs just hours before the delivery truck arrived on Thursday with the flowers Annie had purchased from the flower market in the city. After the flowers were unloaded, they had to be sorted and put into refrigerated storage in the back room. It was a long day, but Friday would prove to be even longer.

It took Annie and Gina all day and well into the night to put all the arrangements together and get everything in its place. Hiring Gina had already proven to be a great decision. Bringing her on board prior to the opening was a stroke of genius, and she had Marie to thank for that. She had convinced Annie that having the help before the opening would allow her and Gina to get to know each other and provide ample time for training before the store opening to the public. Gina had proven to be a quick learner and a hard worker.

Annie always knew that she would have to hire someone to work with her. There was no way she could mind the store, manage the flowers, and make deliveries. She originally considered hiring a delivery driver, but she realized quickly that the deliveries were what started her on this journey and she was not willing to relinquish that job. The truth was she loved delivering joy. She immediately changed her plans to find someone who could manage the customers and help her with the arrangements during her busy times. Annie would continue to make the deliveries, manage the business, and take care of marketing.

Tom and Chad were as busy as she and Gina. They carried the containers of flowers from the refrigerated storage in the back to the work area behind the counter. When the arrangements and bouquets were assembled, they carried the finished products to their new homes in the display cases, countertops, and tables set up around the shop. In their spare time, they placed mini-catalogs for Blooms in hand painted, decorative mailboxes that were strategically placed around the store. Customers could easily find them as they browsed through the store, taking home a free reminder of their visit that included pictures of some of Annie's special arrangements, a price list, and coupons for the Grand Opening specials that would run all month.

The printed materials were all thanks to Chad. He had really come through for Annie with her computer and his suggestions on how to market her store. He was a creative genius. Marie collaborated with Annie on her catalogs by adding advertisements for the café on the back cover and placing Annie's catalogs strategically around her café to increase exposure to Annie's shop. Not surprisingly, that had been one of Chad's brilliant marketing ideas.

The incident with the break-in last month had all but been forgotten. Chad had taken to Tom like a big brother and, since they began working together, Annie had noticed a remarkable change in the boy's attitude. Even Gina commented on the difference she saw in him in just the past few weeks. He had really turned around. Annie was delighted.

"Where do you want me to set up the table for the baked goods?" Betty Lou asked Annie as she came through the back door carrying a large picnic basket.

"Tom has a place set aside for you over there." Annie pointed to a corner of the large work area where Annie created her flower arrangements. "Do you need help carrying anything in?" Annie asked as Betty Lou made her way to the table Annie indicated.

"That would be great if you can spare one of the men," Betty Lou said as she hefted the heavy basket onto the table where she and Lillian would serve up their specialties to customers during the Grand Opening party that would be starting shortly.

"Winnie went to pick up Lillian and they should be here any minute."

About that time Annie heard the sound of Winnie's car horn as she drove down the street, doing her best to draw attention to Annie's shop. Annie just smiled and shook her head, picturing the annoyed look on Lillian's

....

face as she suffered through the stares of everyone looking to see what all the fuss was about.

Tom sent Chad to help Betty Lou while he put the finishing touches on the front area of the store, wiping down surfaces as he made his way around the room. "I think I'll keep you around," Annie said, coming up behind him and putting her arm through his and kissing him lightly.

"I think I'll hold you to that," he said affectionately, pulling her close for a more intimate kiss.

"Um, when you two are done, I need you in the back. There's some guy here with a ton of balloons and he wants to know where to put them," Chad said, trying to pretend he didn't see them kissing.

Tom smiled at Annie and said, "Some day he'll understand."

"Well," Annie chided him with a smile as they headed toward the back, "I promised Scott he wouldn't discover girls on my watch, so we'd better be more discreet next time. If he gets any ideas about being as happy as we are, Scott will never forgive me."

"Forgive you for what?" Scott asked loudly in Annie's ear, sneaking up behind her and startling her with his question.

"Darn it, Scott," Annie exclaimed good-naturedly, "stop doing that!"

"He just can't help himself," Becca explained as if talking about a child. "He'll never grow out of it." She smiled at Scott as he ran to catch up with Tom. As Annie looked around for Angela, Becca assured her that her daughter and her two best friends would be there momentarily.

Angela and her friends, under the supervision of Scott and Becca, would distribute flowers to potential customers in the park across the street. The girls had been working all week to attach business cards to lengths of ribbon that would soon be tied to a variety of fresh flowers to be distributed as advertisement for the shop. Chad's genius strikes again.

While Chad, Tom, and Scott tied daisy-shaped balloons to every possible surface inside and outside the shop, the girls tied the ribbons onto the flowers Annie had prepared. Betty Lou was busy setting up the table where she and Lillian would distribute homemade treats to Annie's customers, and Annie and Becca stepped outside to get a good look at how everything was coming together.

"You did it," Becca said proudly.

"We did it," Annie said to her old friend, knowing she could not have pulled this off without Becca's help.

"Well, what are friends for?" Becca said modestly, hugging her friend close. "This is going to be the best day ever."

"It already is," Annie responded as she hugged her back.

CHAPTER 26

Tom's mother surprised him for a short visit on a sunny afternoon in early August. She was headed to New York and had decided at the last minute to detour for the day to visit her son. The weather was perfect and they decided to walk to town to get a bite to eat. As they strolled down Main Street, they paused frequently to look in the shop windows and comment on the quaint charm of Magnolia Creek. Before Tom knew it, they were walking into Blooms as his mother exclaimed, "This is the most adorable shop! Oh, Tom, I'll only be a moment but I just have to go inside." Tom smiled agreeably at his mother and followed her through the door of Annie's shop.

Kate Walsh went immediately toward the display of fresh sunny daisies that always took center stage in Annie's shop. "Oh my word," she said, "have you ever seen so many beautiful daisies?" She was circling the display for the second time when Annie came out from the back of the shop balancing a large pot of hydrangeas under each arm. Tom quickly reached out to grab the pot closest to him just as it started to sag out of Annie's grip.

"Thank you," she said quickly with a sense of relief, "those were a bit heavier than I thought."

"No problem at all," Tom replied with a smile, kissing Annie lightly on the cheek as she placed the other pot on the counter. Just as Annie turned to ask him what brought him into the shop, she noticed she had a customer.

"Oh my," Tom's mother exclaimed, "look at that! What a gorgeous arrangement. I never would have thought to put these flowers together but they are just lovely."

"I'm glad you like it," Annie said, as the apricot tulips caught Kate's eye.

"Tulips in August? How on earth do you get them to bloom this time of year, and what is that gorgeous color? Oh my goodness, I just love tulips," Kate said to Annie, still moving about the shop as one thing after another drew her attention.

Tom couldn't remember the last time he saw his mother so happy.

Annie turned back to Tom and smiled at him with surprised delight. "Annie, I'd like you to meet my mother, Kate Walsh. Mom, this is Annie Reed, owner and proprietor of Blooms."

"Annie Reed?" Kate asked slowly, momentarily surprised by Tom's introduction.

"It's nice to finally meet you," she said to Annie, recovering her composure quickly, "I've heard so much about you."

....

125

Tom had spoken of Annie several times over the past few months and she suspected her son was falling in love with this young woman. Kate liked Annie instantly. Coupled with what Tom had already told her about Annie, she knew she was a good match for her son. She sincerely hoped for the opportunity to get to know Annie better.

"Why didn't you tell me your mother was in town?" Annie asked Tom when they were alone for a moment in the back of the shop. Annie was wrapping up an arrangement of tulips for Kate to take with her to New York and Tom was enjoying watching her fuss over getting everything just right.

"Why are you so nervous?" he asked her, changing the subject slightly.

"Are you serious?" Annie asked him, pausing for a moment to give him an exasperated look. When he gave her an amused look in return, she had to laugh. "You're right," she admitted "I'm a nervous wreck. Why? Your mother clearly likes me. She thinks I'm some sort of floral savant." Annie joked.

"How could she not like you?" Tom asked her, pulling her close. "Tell me the truth, before you found out she was my mother, you thought she was just a regular customer, didn't you?"

"I did," Annie agreed. "Did you see her? She was all over the place, like a kid in a candy store."

"I honestly don't think I've ever seen her like that," Tom said. "You'd think this was the first time she ever visited a florist."

"Maybe it is," Annie said seriously. "From what you've told me, she always had someone else to do the decorating and party planning, right? Maybe this is the first time that she's actually been in a shop like this, just to browse and enjoy herself."

"Well, if I have anything to say about it, it won't be the last time she visits your shop," Tom said with conviction. "Now, lets get out there and see if we can't convince her to stay for dinner. I'd love for her to get to know you better."

"So what do you think of our little town so far," Annie asked Kate pleasantly. Tom had convinced his mother to stay the night, citing what a great opportunity it would be to get to know Annie better. It didn't take much convincing on his part, his mother was intrigued by what her son had already told her about the woman he obviously loved, and she was anxious to get to know her better.

"Fascinating," Kate replied honestly. The waiter had spent several minutes explaining to Kate what went into many of the unfamiliar Southern specialties served at the Victorian Cafe. Kate considered herself well traveled with a complex and varied palate, and yet she had somehow completely missed Southern cuisine. "I had no idea there were so many ways to use cornmeal and gravy," she said seriously. "But I can't wait to try the honey corn bread; it sounds fabulous!" She smiled at the thought of it.

"After we finished our walk downtown, we took a drive through the country," Tom explained. "I took my mother out past your place so she could see where you get your inspiration," Tom told Annie, obviously proud of all she had accomplished.

"It's a beautiful place, Annie," Kate said enthusiastically. "I can see why flowers are such a big part of your life. Tom tells me that was your grandparents' home until recently. What did you do before moving back to Magnolia Creek?"

"Actually, I was a teacher," Annie replied, "or rather a substitute teacher. After college, I was hoping to stay in Seattle near my family, so I was trying to establish a rapport with a few of the school districts in the area in the hopes of finding a permanent position. Unfortunately, due to budget cuts, full-time teaching positions were hard to come by. So, I was subbing on a pretty regular basis."

"What did you teach?" Kate asked when Annie finished.

"As a substitute teacher I covered a lot of territory, but my interest has always been history," Annie explained, "specifically American history. That's one of the things Tom and I have in common," she said affectionately, smiling at Tom.

"Well, did he ever tell you that I am a member of the Daughters of the American Revolution?" Kate asked Annie, grinning with pride.

"He most certainly did, and I must say I've been looking forward to meeting you," Annie said excitedly. "I have so many questions."

"Well, as much as I love my two favorite women finding so much in common," Tom said appreciatively, "it will have to wait for another time." He nodded toward the waiter making his way to their table. "Our food is here."

CHAPTER 27

"This may be the last cookout of the season," Becca pleaded with Annie, "so you just have to come. Scott will be so disappointed if you and Tom can't make it. He loves talking 'guy stuff' with Tom."

"Okay," Annie said. "I'll talk to Tom and let you know for sure by tomorrow night. Just don't get your hopes up. Tom's been looking forward to this ball game for weeks and I know he doesn't want to disappoint the kids."

For the past several weeks, Tom had been taking the church baseball team to the ball fields at the high school to play teams from other churches in the area. They had started out as casual gatherings for the kids, which gave them something to do on a Saturday afternoon, but had transformed pretty quickly into an informal league among the local churches. Annie knew that Tom got a lot of enjoyment out of spending time with the boys and they with him. She hated to even ask him about cutting it short to go to Scott and Becca's house for a party, but she had promised her friend.

"Why don't you go to the party and I'll join you after the game," Tom offered. He understood Annie's dilemma but was a little disappointed that she had effectively made him the bad guy in the situation.

"I'm sorry Tom," she said again, "I should have just said no. It's just that Becca and Scott have been such good friends to me—to us actually—that I didn't want to disappoint them."

"But that means I'd be letting the kids down, Annie. I don't see a win-win here unless we divide and conquer. As I said, I can join you as soon as the game is over, but I just can't cancel it. Besides," he added for effect, "it's a grudge match between the top two teams and ours is favored to win." He grinned at her, hoping to lessen the sting of his refusal to change his plans.

"Well, we can't have you forfeiting then, can we?" she agreed reluctantly. "I'll just explain the situation to them. After all, they have kids and I know Drew can't wait to be old enough to play ball with the older kids. I'm sure Scott will understand."

Becca and Scott's party was a huge success and Annie was sorry that Tom was missing most of it. She explained repeatedly to everyone who asked that he would be there any time now but that he had made a commitment to the boys at church and he was unwilling to break his promise. Annie had to admit that the later it got, the more it seemed like Tom was breaking the promise he made her to come to the party after the game ended. It was getting dark and she was sure they must be finished by now. She had left two messages on his cell phone already and the later it got the more concerned she became.

"How about I go see if I can find him," Scott offered, trying to put Annie's mind at ease.

She thanked him but declined. "You have guests, Scott, and I'm sure he's fine. It wouldn't be the first time he's left home without his cell phone," Annie explained. What she didn't tell Scott was that Tom had sent her a text earlier that evening from the game to say he loved her and hoped she was having a good time. Something was definitely going on, but she could not imagine what could be keeping him.

Annie left the party a little after nine and drove by the ball fields on the way to Tom's house. There was no one at the park and his car was not in the parking lot. She had no better luck at his house. The house was dark and his car was not in the garage. *Where could he be?* she asked herself, fearing that something bad had happened to him. She decided the best course of action was to go home. Surely he would contact her there.

When she arrived home a short time later, there was no indication that Tom had been there. She went inside and put on the teakettle knowing that would relax her and soothe her nerves while she waited for Tom's call. It turned out she would have a long time to wait.

....

CHAPTER 28

Tom was completely unprepared for the situation he found himself in after the ball game ended.

Ryan had asked to stay over at a friend's house and after a brief conversation with the other boy's mother, Susannah had agreed.

"He's really coming out of his shell," Tom told Susannah. "It's like he's a different kid than when you moved here this summer."

"He is a different kid," Susannah agreed. Small town life agreed with Ryan and she couldn't have been happier. "You know you had a lot to do with it," Susannah said to Tom, opening the conversation as she helped him pack up the equipment.

"What makes you say that?" Tom asked Susannah as he sat on the bench in the dugout, repacking the equipment bags the boys had left behind, eager to join the pastor who was treating them all to pizza in the basement of the church. Tom had offered a long time ago to be responsible for the equipment, donating most of it himself. It was important to him that the boys had the right tools for the job.

He had spent quite a bit of time with these boys and found Ryan to be sweet and engaging when he allowed himself to be. But he still didn't see how he was responsible for the boy's transformation. "It seems like the credit goes to Ryan for being brave enough to try to make friends in a new town," Tom told Susannah. "He jumped in with both feet if you ask me."

"That he did," Susannah agreed, smiling as she remembered how Tom had engaged him in starting a baseball team the very first time they met. "I just meant that Ryan hasn't had a lot of people in his life that he could count on to be there for him." Tom looked up at her, waiting for her to continue. When she didn't, he spoke up.

"Listen, Susannah, I don't know what you and Ryan have been through, but you have a great kid there and he seems to me to be adjusting very well to life here. I hope for his sake that you're planning to stay awhile. I think it would be good for him. He mentioned a few weeks ago that he has lived in several different places but he likes it here the best. I know that I don't know Ryan like you do, but he seemed worried that this may not have been a permanent move and that he may have to leave here someday soon. It's none of my business whatsoever, but I just felt you should know that."

"I appreciate it, Tom, and I assure you that I have no plans to take Ryan away from here. In fact, my plans are quite the opposite. That's what I wanted to talk to you about."

Tom had no idea where this was headed, but he motioned for Susannah to sit down and waited for her to begin. All thoughts of meeting Annie at Scott and Becca's party were forgotten as Susannah began her story.

As Susannah told Tom the real reason she had come to Magnolia Creek, Tom's life turned into a puzzle with pieces that he just couldn't seem to make fit. He wanted them all to fit; in fact, he was convinced he could force them to fit, but he just didn't yet know how. All he knew for certain that evening was that his life had changed forever, and definitely for the better.

"I'm not actually Ryan's biological mother," Susannah began slowly. "I'm his aunt. His mother passed away several years ago after battling a long illness."

"I'm so sorry for your loss," Tom said automatically, surprised by Susannah's statement that she wasn't Ryan's mother. "That must have been incredibly hard on both of you," he added sincerely.

"My sister's name was Maggie Davidson, Tom," Susannah continued quickly and then paused to let her words sink in.

"Maggie?" he asked her, a confused look on his face. "My Maggie is your sister?"

"Was," she corrected him gently, "she was my sister. And Ryan is her son. Your son."

"He's my son?" Tom said in amazement. "Ryan is mine?" He knew he was repeating himself, but he just couldn't believe what he was hearing.

"Yes," Susannah assured him, watching him carefully to see his reaction. Her plans hinged completely on

Tom's acceptance of Ryan as his son and his willingness to take on the joy and responsibility of being Ryan's dad. She hadn't gotten to that part, yet. She was just giving Tom time to get his head around the fact that he had a son and that son was Ryan.

"Sweet, engaging, courageous Ryan. Wow, talk about a game-changer! I'm a dad," Tom said aloud. Again.

Susannah broke into a wide grin and tears came to her eyes as she nodded emphatically that yes, Tom was indeed a dad. As the news finally sunk in and filled Tom with amazement and joy, he reached out and hugged Susannah, lifting her completely off the dugout bench.

"Sorry," he apologized as he let her down, "I hope I didn't overstep. I'm just so excited I don't know what to do with myself." He began to pace as Susannah sat back down to wait until he was ready to hear the rest. Tom's pacing slowed as it dawned on him that he and Ryan were not the only people in this story.

"I'm really sorry about Maggie," Tom said quietly as he stopped his pacing and looked compassionately at Susannah. "I know your sister and I had our differences, but I did love her and I can't even imagine how hard her death must have been on you and your family."

"Thank you, Tom," Susannah replied. "And I hope you understand why it took me so long to reach out to you. Ryan was only five when he lost his mother, but she had been sick for as long as he can remember. My parents and I did not agree with Maggie's decision to keep her pregnancy from you, but we felt it was her decision to make and in light of the short-lived marriage and the subsequent divorce, we decided to respect her wishes."

"Maggie arranged for me to have sole custody of Ryan upon her death," Susannah continued, "and in fact he lived with me for almost a year while she was confined to the hospital. Maggie talked openly with Ryan about what would happen after she went to heaven, preparing him as much as she could for what was to come."

"So what now?" Tom asked. "I take it that the reason we're having this conversation alone is that Ryan doesn't know that I'm his dad."

"No, he doesn't," Susannah said honestly. "In fact, we haven't ever had a conversation about his dad, I mean you. I do have his birth certificate naming you as the father and I am certainly willing to do whatever you wish to prove paternity. Tom, I know this is a lot to digest, and I want to make this transition as easy as possible for all of us. So lets talk again when you've had time to think about it."

"What transition?" Tom asked Susannah pointedly. "You said you were planning to stay in Magnolia Creek."

"No, Tom, I said I have no intention of taking Ryan away from here, away from you. My intention has always been to reunite father and son. And now, after meeting you and seeing how the two of you have bonded, I am more convinced than ever that it's the best thing for Ryan.

"Tom, I have been Ryan's sole guardian since his mother went into the hospital when he was just four years old. I will always be his aunt, but I believe the privilege of caring for your son belongs to you now."

It was almost nine as Tom walked Susannah to her car. They agreed to meet again the next day after Susannah's shift at the café ended to discuss what to do next. Tom loaded the equipment bags into his trunk and began to drive, thinking about what he had just learned.

He needed to talk to Annie, but he just wasn't ready. Things were going so well between them. He loved her deeply, but they had not yet talked about the future in terms of marriage or children. He suspected they would both want to stay in Magnolia Creek as they had each come to think of it as home, but bringing a child into the relationship at this point? He would definitely have to figure out the best way to tell her. After all, he had not even told her that he had been married before. And now he was a package deal, father and son. He definitely needed to think about how to approach this in the right way. There were two things he knew for sure, Tom decided. He wanted his son and he wanted Annie. He would have to tread lightly with them both, as he couldn't risk losing either one of them.

CHAPTER 29

It was after midnight when Tom pulled into Annie's driveway. He found lights on in the kitchen, but Annie did not respond when he called her name. Tom checked the downstairs first but didn't see her. He made his way upstairs to see if she had gone to bed without locking up. Her bed was made and she was nowhere to be found. As he entered the guest room and reached for the light, he noticed lights on in the barn. As he looked closer, he could make out Annie's silhouette moving around in the greenhouse.

"Annie?" Tom called as he made his way around the house to the backyard. "Annie?" he called again as he entered the barn, heading toward the door that led into the greenhouse.

"I'm in here, Tom," Annie replied evenly from the far corner of the greenhouse. "I'll be out in just a second." It would have been difficult for him to get to her in there, especially with only the growing lamps on as Annie had every nook and cranny filled with flowers.

"Are you all right, Tom?" she asked with concern, as soon as she came through the doorway a moment later, wiping her dirty hands on her smock.

"I'm fine, Annie," Tom began, "and I'm really sorry about tonight."

"Well," Annie began sarcastically, "as long as you're sorry, I guess its okay. Okay that I was sick with worry that something had happened to you. Okay that I actually called the hospital an hour ago because I literally could not imagine a scenario where you were not dead in a ditch somewhere or lying unconscious in the emergency room, fighting for your life. Okay that..." Annie choked on her tears and could not continue.

Tom started toward her to comfort her, but she held up her hand as she composed herself. "No! Don't you dare try to make it all better by patting my head and wiping my tears. By telling me I'm overreacting and that I need to calm down. Don't you dare!" she shouted, completely losing control.

It only took Tom a moment to realize that she was slowly starting to sink to the floor and he closed the gap between them in seconds to catch her and lower her gently to the bench just outside the greenhouse door. She pushed him away, sobbing into her hands, hiding her face from him. Tom had never felt so helpless. He wanted to comfort her and assure her that everything was fine, but he couldn't. She wouldn't let him near her. And in reality everything was not fine. In fact, fine was not even on the horizon that night. Tom had no idea what to do at that moment, but he knew he could not leave Annie so he sat down on the floor of the barn and waited. He waited for Annie to let him explain. He needed her to know how much he loved her and how insensitive he had been to not call and let her know he was okay.

The truth was that Tom was so shaken by Susannah's news that he had never even thought of how Annie would feel when he didn't show up for the party. She had every right to be angry with him. His insensitivity had hurt her deeply. He should have known that Annie would be worried because she loved him. But he needed her to know what happened and why he didn't call. Couldn't she see that he was struggling with his own news? News he needed to share with her?

Tom tried again to talk to Annie but to no avail. She simply got up from the bench, hung up her dirty smock on a hook above her head, walked past Tom and out of the barn without a word. She walked straight into the house, closed the door, turned off the light, and went to bed.

He can sit there all night for all I care, she thought to herself as she collapsed on her bed and once again began to cry.

Tom sat there and watched Annie walk out without a word. He was stunned at her actions and decided that if that was how she was going to act then she could wallow in her tears. He wasn't going to beg for her to listen to what he had to say. *Besides*, he thought as he stood up and headed for the door, *I have more pressing matters to think about before my meeting with Susannah tomorrow evening.* Lots of things to think about, it seemed to him now.

....

CHAPTER 30

"What happened?" Becca asked Annie when she saw her at church the next morning. "Annie," she asked again, "what happened last night? Are you okay?"

"I don't want to see him, Becca," Annie announced to her friend. "If you see him heading this way, you have to change seats with me. I do *not* want to talk to him."

"Annie," Becca pleaded, "what is going on? Everything was going so well for you two. This isn't about him choosing the game over the party, is it? Oh, Annie, I hope not. I wouldn't want something as silly as a party to come between you two. You're meant to be together, I just know it."

"No, it wasn't the party. At least not directly," Annie explained. "It's the fact that Tom showed up at my house at midnight without so much as a call to let me know he was okay. I mean what was he thinking? He was supposed to come to the party after the game. I know the game should have been over well before seven as the kids were having pizza afterward with some of the church staff. I even drove by the ball fields when I left your house and that was well after nine. I was really getting worried so I went by his house. He wasn't home either, so I decided I'd better go home in case he tried to reach me there.

"Oh, Becca, I was so worried that something happened to him that I actually called the hospital just to check to see if he had been in an accident!" Annie said, ashamed of her vulnerability.

"Oh, Annie, I'm so sorry," Becca said sympathetically. "I had no idea you were going through all that last night. No wonder you're so upset. Why was he so late?"

"No idea," Annie said coldly.

"What do you mean?" Becca pressed. "I thought you said he came by around midnight. What on earth did he have to say for why he stood you up?"

"Does it matter?" Annie asked sarcastically, not meeting Becca's eye, ashamed of how she was feeling. "The fact is that he did stand me up and never even bothered to call. I felt like an idiot calling the hospital when they told me he wasn't there. What kind of woman tries to track down her boyfriend in the middle of the night? They must have thought I was pathetic. Not even able to keep track of my own boyfriend on a Saturday night. 'Pathetic' is what I am." Annie felt the hurt and shame bubbling up inside her again. She realized now that coming here was a bad idea. She couldn't face running into Tom, not yet. Not until she could get her emotions under control.

Annie looked up at Becca to tell her she was going to leave when she realized that Tom must have been standing behind her as she spoke to her friend. Becca looked back down at her with concern in her eyes as Tom spoke.

"Good morning, Annie," he said formally. "I trust you slept well." He regretted it as soon as he said it, but it was too late. Annie got up from her seat without turning around and excused herself from the pew. Before Tom could follow her, the music began and everyone stood for the first hymn. Tom apologized to Scott and Becca and made his way through the crowd to the exit. Annie was nowhere to be seen. He cursed his lack of control and made his way to his car. He sat there until the service was over, hoping to see Annie return to her friends. Hoping for another chance to explain what happened and apologize for hurting her.

Annie could see Tom in his car from where she was sitting in the area of the attic above the kitchen. She and Becca had claimed that area as their secret space when they were little girls. Annie made her way there almost without thinking when she ran from the church to avoid Tom. She knew she was overreacting. She was ashamed of how callous she was treating Tom, the man she said she loved, but she just couldn't seem to stop. She felt like a spoiled child punishing him for something he was trying to apologize for. And why? *Why can I not let this go?* she wondered. Yes, he had been wrong not to call her. He had been insensitive to let her worry about him. Didn't he realize how much she loved him? Didn't he understand her fear of losing him?

As Annie sat there hugging her knees, watching Tom as he sat in the car, waiting for a chance to talk to

....

her, she realized that she was preventing exactly what she was hoping for. She loved Tom and she did not want to lose him. And yet her actions since the first time he came to her to explain had been to push him away. It was time to grow up and hear what he had to say.

Annie headed down the back staircase and snuck out the door without being seen. As she rounded the side of the building, she noticed Tom's car was no longer in the lot. He must have driven off while she was making her way down from the attic. She had to admit, he'd waited a lot longer than she expected, especially given the way she had spoken of him to Becca.

Tom decided he needed a diversion. He was meeting with Susannah at 5:00 p.m. when her shift ended at the café. When Annie didn't show at the church, he had gone home to do some work in the garden to try to take his mind off her. A few hours of turning soil and pulling stalks from the large garden in the backyard had done wonders for his attitude. Tom loved working with his hands and looked forward to teaching Ryan about gardening, plumbing, fixing a roof, and all the other invaluable lessons he never learned from his dad.

As he drove to the café, he thought he would suggest they all go out for pizza. The local pizzeria had an arcade that the kids loved and it would keep Ryan busy, allowing him to talk with Susannah about how to proceed with the change of custody. Neither of them wanted to rush the process. They had not yet revealed to Ryan that Tom was his father, but they both felt it was prudent to make plans.

When Tom met up with Susannah outside the café, he suggested the pizzeria. "That's very thoughtful of you, Tom, and I know Ryan would love the arcade, but I had hoped that you would come to our house for dinner tonight."

"Of course," Tom said, "whatever works best for you."

"Great," Susannah said brightly, "I'll swing by and pick up Ryan at the sitter's house and I'll meet you at my place shortly. I put a roast in the slow cooker this morning so we should be ready to eat by six. I just have to heat up the biscuits I got from the café and we'll be all set."

Tom took the long way to Susannah's house, which meant he drove downtown to pass by Blooms on his way. He intended to give Susannah time to pick up Ryan from the sitter's house and get home before he arrived, but he realized as he parked in front of the shop that this detour was more about Annie than about Susannah.

"How could I have been so oblivious to her feelings?" he wondered aloud as he sat in his car looking at the shop windows. She was so full of life and love and joy. *That's it exactly,* Tom thought. Annie was joyful. But that was not the woman he saw last night in the barn, and it was definitely not the woman he heard in church this morning. What he just couldn't reconcile in his mind was how it had gone so wrong so fast. He was more than willing to admit his part in this, but what had happened to cause Annie to react so uncharacteristically cold? *I just don't get it,* he thought as he pulled away from the curb to try to reconcile another part of his life that had recently taken him by surprise—fatherhood.

"Tom!" Ryan exclaimed as he opened the door to Tom's knock. "Mom! Mom! Tom's here!" Ryan yelled excitedly as he ran into the kitchen to let Susannah know their guest had arrived.

"Okay," she said calmly, "I'm coming." Susannah put the biscuits in the oven and went into the living room to greet their guest.

"Hi Tom," she said, motioning with her hand for him to come into the living room and have a seat. "Ryan, would you see if Tom would like a glass of water or some sweet tea?"

Tom indicated that sweet tea would be great and Ryan rushed off to the kitchen to get it for him.

"Just in case you couldn't tell, he's very excited that you came for dinner." Susannah smiled at Tom as he took his seat. "He didn't ask why you were coming for dinner," she whispered to Tom while Ryan was still in the kitchen, "so I didn't offer an explanation."

"I wondered about that on the way over here," Tom said in a quiet voice. "Maybe we could say that you offered me a home-cooked meal and I would have been a fool to say no."

"Sounds good," she said softly, "simple yet elegant."

The evening could not have gone better from Tom's perspective. The food was delicious and Susannah insisted that Ryan show Tom around while she did the dishes. Ryan started with his bedroom, which turned out to be full of sports equipment and posters of his favorite athletes. Tom could not have been happier and was already looking forward to sharing his love of sports with his son.

Next, Ryan took Tom into the backyard to show him the rest of his gear. When he was done with the tour, Tom suggested Ryan grab a basketball and they proceeded to shoot hoops until Susannah called them in for dessert.

"This was the best night ever," Ryan told Susannah as she tucked him into bed and kissed him goodnight.

"You really like Tom, don't you, honey?" she asked him as she started out the door.

"Uh-huh," Ryan answered sleepily as she turned off the light, "he likes baseball, just like me."

"Well, that seals it," Susannah said, returning from putting Ryan to bed. "You're a hit. Apparently the baseball fan angle worked."

"What angle?" Tom asked innocently. "I love baseball! I used to beg my father to take me to a game, but he never did. He'd drag me along to business meetings when I was older, so I could 'learn how the game is played.' His words, not mine by the way. But he never once took me to a real game. Not even polo." Tom laughed at his own joke.

"Well, it sounds to me like Ryan won't have to worry about that, will he?" Susannah asked with no attempt at hiding the real question.

"No, I don't suppose he will." Tom smiled. "So tell me how this works, Susannah. You've had a lot more time to work this out than I have so where do we go from here?"

"Are you really ready for this, Tom? I know you and Annie are pretty serious but you haven't mentioned her at all since we talked last night. How did she take the news?"

"I haven't told her yet," Tom admitted.

"Why on earth not?" Susannah asked, stunned at his response. "I'm sorry if you feel that I'm prying, Tom, but we're talking about family here and I don't think that your relationship with Annie is off limits to our discussion. I expect it will have a direct impact on Ryan and I need to know if she is on board."

"I agree completely, Susannah. It's just that when I didn't show up to meet her last night, she got so worried she called the hospital to see if I'd been in an accident."

"Oh no," Susannah said, concerned that her choice of timing to talk to Tom had caused a problem in their relationship.

"I know I should have called her, and I tried to explain later that evening, but by then she was so upset she just couldn't hear me. I tried again today, but I think she needs more time. I will make it right, Susannah," he promised. "I love Annie and I have no intention of letting her go."

"And what if she refuses to accept Ryan," Susannah asked pointedly, "whom will you choose then?"

CHAPTER 31

"So, are you going to tell me what's bothering you, Annie, or do I have to pry it out of you?" Lillian asked as they sat in a secluded corner of the patio, enjoying the morning sun.

Annie had stopped by unexpectedly to visit with her friend and Lillian could see she needed to talk.

"I'm such a fool," Annie began, tears welling up in her eyes.

"You can stop right there!" Lillian said firmly, startling Annie with her tone. "You are no fool, Annie Reed, and I will not listen to you or anyone else say that you are. Now"—she smiled slightly and softened her tone—"why don't you start from the beginning?"

Annie took her time and relayed the events of the weekend to Lillian, answering her questions honestly and providing more details as requested. She had never told anyone the details of her last boyfriend's betrayal, not even her mother. But as she relayed the events of the weekend to Lillian, it became obvious to Annie that her fear of being played for a fool had been at the root of her anger with Tom. She was literally punishing him for something that Jarrod did. "So what should I do?" Annie asked Lillian when she had finished her story.

"I think you know what to do, Annie," Lillian said calmly.

"I need to apologize to Tom and beg him to forgive my appalling behavior."

"Apologize to him," Lillian corrected her patiently, "explain your behavior, remind him how much you love him, and tell him that you are ready to hear what he has to say."

"Don't just sit there and nod your head at me, young lady, listen to what I'm telling you. Your appalling behavior, your word by the way, not mine, was based on events in your past that you have not yet shared with Tom. He has no basis to understand where his behavior took you emotionally. You owe it to him and to yourself," Lillian continued, "to help him understand what happened. It's the only way to ensure this type of misunderstanding doesn't happen again. I can tell you from vast experience, Annie, that he will disappoint you again, just as you will disappoint him from time to time. It's inevitable, but it doesn't have to ruin what you two have together."

"Understanding and accepting each other's weaknesses and vulnerabilities is what brings you closer together and deepens the love you already share. That's true love, Annie, the kind that lasts a lifetime. It's not about finding perfection but rather about understanding and acceptance."

"Annie!" Tom called her name loudly as he knocked on her front door. "Open the door Annie, we need to talk."

"I agree," Annie replied calmly as she opened the door to let him in. "Can I get you anything?"

"No thanks, Annie," he said. "I'm fine." As she turned to join him on the sofa, he said, "Actually, there is one thing I need from you." He took her by the hand and slowly pulled her into his lap. He hugged her to him until he felt her body meld with his. As he held her close, he felt her weeping softly into his chest. He continued to hold her until she stopped, then he lifted her face to kiss her softly and wipe away her tears.

After a few moments, Annie moved to sit beside him on the sofa. "Tom, I'm sorry for the way I behaved toward you and I think it's important that you know why. There's something I'd like to share with you."

"Okay, Annie," Tom said. "There's something I want to share with you as well. Why don't you start?"

Annie began by explaining to Tom about the relationship she had mentioned to him on their trip back from the beach. She shared the circumstances around Jarrod's betrayal of her trust in him and the humiliation and pain that resurfaced during the incident with Tom on Saturday night.

Tom listened intently to Annie's description of the events that shaped her life without interrupting, except to place his hand on her knee when she faltered in the retelling. When she finished explaining why she reacted the way she did and how she now knew that she was punishing Tom for something he didn't do, she reminded him that she loved him deeply and how that love made her vulnerable to be hurt again.

"But," she said boldly, "I know you, Tom Walsh, and I know you would not intentionally hurt me. I trust you with my heart. All of it. If you can forgive me I really would like to hear what you tried to tell me that night."

"Of course I forgive you, Annie, I love you. And I want you to know how deeply sorry I am that I was the cause of your pain. I don't ever want to put you through that again. You're everything to me, Annie. In fact, until two days ago I could barely remember my life before I met you. Nor did I want to. I had everything I wanted right here in Magnolia Creek. And then on Saturday evening after the ball game with the kids, I had a conversation with Susannah Davidson that changed my life forever."

"Before I get into that, Annie, I too need to share with you a part of my history that I have not yet told you about. I was married once before," Tom began, "*very* briefly."

As he told Annie about his brief relationship and even shorter marriage to Maggie, Tom explained that Susannah was Maggie's sister. He had never actually met any of Maggie's family as she had moved to California to escape the oppression she felt was being unfairly inflicted on her by her controlling parents. Tom understood her need for freedom and they thought they had each found their soul mate. Reality settled in quickly and they both realized the marriage was hasty and borne out of rebellion against their families. They decided to divorce quietly in Reno and get on with their lives.

"What I didn't know until Saturday," he explained, taking Annie's hands in his and watching her closely, "was that Maggie was pregnant when we split up." Annie's eyes widened but she did not stop him. "She never told me, Annie."

He continued the story as Susannah had explained it to him. "Had she not gotten sick, I might never have known I have a son. Ryan is *my* son, Annie. Susannah came here intentionally to meet me to determine if I was fit to be Ryan's dad." He allowed Annie a moment to absorb what he just said before continuing. "That's the reason I didn't call you that night Annie, I just needed time to think. I'm so sorry I hurt you."

"You have a son. Sweet, adorable, brave little Ryan Davidson is *your* son. Tom, I think that is the most wonderful news I have ever heard!" she exclaimed and leapt into his arms, full of joy.

Tom knew without a doubt that he loved Annie Reed and that he wanted to spend the rest of his life with her, but he had not truly realized the depth of that love until that very moment.

CHAPTER 32

"So how come you don't have any kids?" Ryan asked Tom as he passed him the potatoes.

Tom was at a loss for words, completely taken off guard by the question from his own son. "That's a good question, Ryan," Tom answered slowly, looking at Susannah for help.

"It may very well be a good question," Susannah said to Ryan, "but it's rude to ask. Perhaps Tom doesn't wish to talk about his family with us, so we'll let him tell us if and when he's ready."

"Yes, ma'am," Ryan said dejectedly, adding, "but he said it was a good question," under his breath. Much to Tom's relief, Susannah quickly changed the subject.

When they had finished dinner, Susannah sent Ryan outside but asked Tom to help her with clearing the table, giving them a few moments to speak privately.

"I know it's soon, Tom, but if he asks again, and I suspect he will, I think he's ready to know the truth. In fact, he almost stumbled on it himself this afternoon when he made the connection that your name is the same as his father's. I had no idea Maggie had told him your first name. He was so excited about you coming over, I almost told him right then."

"I'm glad you didn't," Tom said thankfully. "I just feel like it's something he should hear from me."

"I know," Susannah said quickly, "and my parents and I agree with you. It just came as a shock to hear him say so casually, 'his name is Tom, too. Just like our Tom,'" she repeated as they laughed at the absurdity of the situation.

Tom headed outside to help Ryan with his pitching as promised. "So, do you have a girlfriend, Ryan?" Tom asked as he repositioned his son's arm to give him more power and accuracy.

"No," Ryan answered, "not anymore anyway. Not since we moved here. I don't really know many girls."

"Hmmm," Tom said thoughtfully, "that's too bad. There are a lot of nice girls in Magnolia Creek. I'm sure you'll have several to choose from. If you're interested, that is."

"I don't know," Ryan answered, concentrating on his posture, "girls can be a lot of work."

"You've got that right, son!" Tom exclaimed with a laugh, thinking of the misunderstanding with Annie and not aware that he had just called Ryan *son*. When he realized it a moment later, he recovered quickly by asking Ryan what he thought of Annie.

"I like her," Ryan said without hesitation. "She's pretty cool for a grown-up and she's always really nice to the kids at church. One time she even brought ice cream for all the kids after Sunday school. That was so great!"

"And she's pretty, right?" Tom asked with a grin.

"Yeah," Ryan agreed, giving Tom a big grin, "she's pretty."

"So are you going to marry her?" Ryan asked a few minutes later, completely stopping what he was doing to look at Tom.

"Someday," Tom replied, "if I'm lucky."

"Oh," Ryan said, turning back to his pitching.

"I thought you liked Annie," Tom said to him, trying to engage him further.

"I do like her," Ryan answered. "It's just that, well, I thought maybe you liked my mom, too."

"I see," Tom said quietly, understanding that Ryan was unsure of his role in Tom's life if he married Annie.

"Lets take a break for a minute, Ryan," Tom said, turning to sit on the edge of the porch. "I'd like to talk to you man to man."

Ryan came and sat beside Tom, his legs not quite reaching the ground. "I think it's important to make sure a man knows where he stands, don't you?" Tom began.

"Uh-huh," Ryan replied.

"I love Annie and even though I haven't actually asked her yet, I do intend to marry her. I think it's important for you to know that won't change anything between us."

"In fact," he continued as Ryan smiled at him, clearly relieved, "you couldn't get rid of me if you tried."

Tom reached out to put his arm around Ryan and the boy hugged him tightly. *Life is good*, Tom thought at that moment.

"I think the next step is to start planting the seeds with Ryan that maybe it would be a good idea for us to look for his father."

"No," Tom disagreed with Susannah, "I think we need to be honest with him. He's a bright kid and I don't want him to feel like we're keeping this from him any longer. You know him better than I do, at least for now, but he is my son and I don't want him to have to wait any longer to know he has a father who loves him and wants him. He needs to know that Maggie never told me she was pregnant and I never knew about him until a few days ago. It's important that he knows that I didn't reject him or his mother. I couldn't stand it if he thought I chose to leave him."

"Okay then," Susannah said with a smile, happy to relinquish this task to Tom. "When are you going to tell him?"

"Tomorrow," Tom said suddenly, ready to have this behind them so they could get on with their lives.

"Okay," Susannah agreed, "but I think it would be best if we figured out how this is going to work before we break the news to him that he will be staying here with his father when I move back to Philadelphia."

"What do you mean?" Tom asked Susannah, confused by her statement that she would not be staying. "You never said anything about leaving town."

"Well, we never got around to the details, did we, Tom? It's for the best," she explained. "Really it is. While my parents and I will always be his family, he needs to adjust to his new life with you. I believe that will be much harder for all of us if I am living down the street, don't you agree?"

Tom didn't know what to think. The reality was settling in that in spite of his excitement of finding out that Ryan was his son, there were logistics to consider and lives besides his and Ryan's that were impacted by these decisions. He needed to talk to Annie.

CHAPTER 33

The weather was unseasonably warm for Labor Day and they all agreed to have a cookout at Annie's house to celebrate the end of summer and the kid's return to school. Ryan would be starting the third grade this year and Annie had invited several of his friends from the church baseball team over to make it a special day for him.

Tom, Annie, and Susannah had agreed that when the party was over, they would sit down with Ryan and tell him the truth about Tom and his mother and how they ended up in Magnolia Creek.

"Tom, I think you should follow your instincts when it comes to Ryan," Annie advised him as they sat at her kitchen table discussing his upcoming talk with Ryan. "From day one you have shared a special bond with that boy, long before you knew he was your son. Trust that and you'll do fine. He idolizes you, Tom, and with good reason. You are genuine, caring, fun, and you love baseball as much as he does. How could he not be thrilled to find out you're his dad?"

"I appreciate your optimism Annie, but I'm worried that Ryan might end up resenting me for not being there for the first eight years of his life. The years he could have really used a dad to help him through his mother's illness and her death. What could I say then that would make any difference at all? "I didn't know about you then" seems so lame."

"I'm sure you'll know what to say *if* that time comes, Tom. In the meantime, focus on the fact that you have an incredible son and Ryan has the absolute best dad he could ever hope for."

"Thanks, Annie. I needed to hear that."

"Well, if you need any more encouragement, you're about to get it. I think I heard Winnie's car pull in a minute ago so we should be getting company right about…"

"Hello," Betty Lou said loudly, coming up the front porch steps.

"Anyone home?" Winnie called through the screen door.

"Come on in," Annie called back, giving Tom an affectionate kiss as she rose from her seat at the table, "we're in the kitchen."

"Why so serious?" Winnie asked as she and Betty Lou came into the kitchen carrying large bowls of homemade potato salad and coleslaw for the party.

"Today is the day I get to tell Ryan that I'm his father," Tom explained as he took the bowls from the women and put them in the fridge.

"Then it's a great day, right?" Winnie asked, a little confused.

"It absolutely is," Tom agreed quickly, "it's just that, well, I don't know how he's going to take the news. I guess I'm concerned about him being upset that I wasn't there for him when he needed me" Tom explained, "like when his mother died."

"Sit down here for a minute, Tom." Betty Lou indicated the chair he had vacated moments earlier after his conversation with Annie on this very subject. "Let me tell you a story about a boy and his father that I think may shed some light on this for you."

"There was a young boy named Joseph," Betty Lou began as she sat next to Tom, "who was sold into slavery by his jealous brothers. The brothers lied to their father, telling him that a wild animal had eaten his beloved son. He was devastated. He loved his son deeply and thought he would never again feel joy. The brothers made a pact to take their secret to the grave, never expecting to see Joseph again. But that was not to be."

Tom smiled knowingly at Annie as Betty Lou paused for effect.

"Many years later, the brothers were confronted by their youngest sibling, alive and well mind you, and in a position of power. Joseph quickly learned that his beloved father was still alive. The brothers were instructed to bring their father to him. You see, he loved his father deeply and knew that his father loved him, too. They were reunited and both men were overjoyed to learn that the other lived. There was no animosity or accusations, not even toward the treacherous brothers.

The son learned that his father had been deceived, and the father learned that his son had been betrayed. But their joy at being reunited was all that mattered to them." Betty Lou sat back and let her last statement sink in.

"I see what you mean," Tom said to her, "you think that Ryan will be so happy to learn that I'm his father, the rest won't matter."

"Exactly," Betty Lou said earnestly. "Besides, he's only eight," she added with a wink, "not fifteen!"

"Point taken," Tom said as he rose from the table, helping the older woman to her feet. "Thank you, Betty Lou. I feel better already. You're quite a storyteller." She smiled up at him as he hugged her warmly.

CHAPTER 34

It was a beautiful day and the party was a big success. After all of the guest left, Ryan and Tom relaxed on the front porch while Annie and Susannah cleaned up and prepared for their talk with Ryan.

"I have to admit," Annie said to Susannah as they dried and put away dishes, "that while I know it sounds selfish, I am worried that Ryan will resent me when he realizes that staying with his dad means losing you."

"It's not selfish, Annie," Susannah reassured her. "I worried about the same thing. It's why I've always been very clear with Ryan that my relationship with Tom is all about him, and not about Tom and me."

"Ryan loves you, Annie, and he loves Tom. I know staying here with Tom is what's best for him. He needs a father. That's what I never understood about Maggie's decision to keep this from Tom in the first place. You would think that growing up without a father herself when she was so young would have caused her to seek out Tom, for Ryan's sake."

"I'm confused," Annie admitted. "I thought Maggie was your sister."

"She is, or rather was," Susannah corrected herself, "my half sister. Our mother met my father when she and Maggie moved to Philadelphia. Maggie was four at the time and I was born a year later. Never once did Mother talk to us about Maggie's biological father. Apparently they left in the middle of the night one night and she never looked back. I have no idea why, but Maggie told me once that whenever she asked about her real dad, Mother would tell her, 'Frederick is your father now.' Maggie told me that eventually she just stopped asking."

The talk with Ryan could not have gone any better if it were a Hollywood movie, scripted to have a happy ending. To say Ryan was ecstatic was an understatement. Tom sat down with him first, alone in the living room, and began to tell him about his conversation with Susannah merely a week before. He had decided that the direct approach was the right one.

"I need to talk to you," Tom said to Ryan as they sat together on Annie's large overstuffed sofa. "It's kind of important," he added, glancing at him, "it's about your mother."

"My mother?" Ryan asked, looking at Tom quizzically, unsure of where this was headed.

"Ryan, Susannah told me that she is really your aunt."

"She did?"

"Yes, she did. And she also told me that your mother passed away," he added softly.

Ryan kept his eyes on his shoes as he thought about what Tom had just said.

"Did your mother ever talk to you about your father, Ryan?" Tom asked gently, watching closely for his reaction.

"Not really," he replied evenly, "just that they got a divorce before I was born and that his name is Tom, too. Just like you."

"Exactly like me," Tom smiled broadly as he watched the realization cross Ryan's face.

"Do you mean," Ryan paused, looking at Tom with wonder, "are you my dad?"

"I am," Tom said with pride. "Is that okay?"

Annie and Susannah had just made their way quietly into the room when they saw Ryan's eyes grow large as he learned that Tom Walsh was in fact his father.

He then jumped up and began to run around the room shouting, "Yes! Yes! Yes!" and pumping his fists in the air. Tom looked at Annie and then at Susannah, shrugged his shoulders in amazement, and broke into a huge grin.

In the next moment, Tom had joined his son running around the living room shouting, "Yes! Yes! Yes!" and pumping *his* fists in the air. The women laughed with joy and relief as Tom picked up Ryan and held him up, shouting, "This is my son! MY SON!"

An hour later both Ryan and Tom were sound asleep on the sofa, Ryan's head on a pillow in Tom's lap and clutching the arm that Tom had draped over his chest.

"I have to capture this moment," Annie told Susannah cheerfully as she snapped the first of many pictures of father and son.

A short while later, Tom carried an exhausted Ryan to Susannah's car, promising to come by in the morning for some pitching practice. Ryan had not yet had time to process what would happen next and Tom did not want to rush that conversation. They had made it through the first hurdle, but this was far from over. Ryan's life would change when he came to live with Tom, but before that could happen there were legal issues to settle and he had to be sure Ryan was ready to deal with his aunt returning to her home in Philadelphia.

As far as Tom was concerned, they had all the time in the world to make this work. He wasn't going anywhere.

CHAPTER 35

"I think he's ready, don't you?" Susannah asked Tom as they left Ryan's school. Tonight had been the last parent-teacher conference of the year as the holidays were already upon them.

"I can't believe how fast the past few months have gone by," Tom said as they made their way to his car. It seems like just last week that we brought Ryan here for his first day of school. The memory of Ryan proudly introducing him as his dad was one Tom thought he'd never forget.

"Well that's because you have a very active eight year old practically living with you, keeping you on your toes. Speaking of which," she added quickly, "I think it's time we made it permanent, don't you? I mean Ryan is at your place more than mine most of the time and he seems very comfortable there."

"I think so, too" Tom agreed, "but shouldn't we let him decide when he's ready? I mean, it's not like you're going anywhere, right?"

"Actually, I am," Susannah said with a sideling glance at Tom as he drove her home.

"What do you mean? Are you going somewhere for the holidays?" Tom pressed, "I don't know if that's a good idea. I know Ryan really wants you to be here for Christmas and Annie's planning a big party."

"Oh no, I'll be here for the holidays," she assured him, "but I'm not planning to stay in Magnolia Creek forever, Tom. My plan has always been to reunite the two of you and then return home to Philadelphia."

Does Ryan know? I think it's important that we are honest with him."

"He does know, and he understands that his life is here with you and my life is in Philadelphia with his grandparents. He'll be fine, Tom, really. I'll be here for the holidays and after that I'll call him and he can call me. You and I can work out times during his school breaks that we can schedule visits."

"I'm just surprised he's never mentioned it," Tom said, "but I guess that's a good thing. If he was worried about you leaving, he definitely would have told me about it."

"Exactly. Listen, I do have a favor to ask of you. I've decided to keep the rental house through the end of the year so I have somewhere to stay when I'm here for Christmas. It also gives me a sense of comfort that Ryan will know that I'm coming back, at least one more time. Would you mind just keeping an eye on it for me while I'm gone?"

"No problem at all," Tom assured her, as he looked forward to having Ryan living with him full time. The

legal documents had been finalized for several weeks—
they were just giving Ryan time to make the transition
from his aunt to his father.

CHAPTER 36

"So?" Tom asked Ryan expectantly. "What do you think?"

"Oh man, Dad, Annie's going to freak out when she sees that!" Ryan exclaimed with enthusiasm.

"I sure hope so," Tom said, his nervousness increasing as the big day approached.

He and Ryan had talked at great length about Tom proposing to Annie and what the best way would be for them to ask her to join their family. Ryan had been the one to suggest a joint proposal and Tom had decided that Christmas Eve would be the best time to ask her. They would wait until the party was over and they had all returned from the candlelight service at church. After everyone left and Annie's parents went to bed, Tom would ask Annie to join him in the living room by the fireplace where he and Ryan would pop the question, or questions to be more accurate.

"Aunt Susannah!" Ryan exclaimed when he picked up the phone. "When are you coming back? It's almost Christmas! You said you were coming back for

Christmas and I need you to take me shopping for Dad and Annie. You promised you would. You are coming back soon, aren't you?"

"Yes, Ryan," Susannah said as soon as he finished. "I'll be back next weekend. That's a whole week before Christmas so we'll have plenty of time to shop. I promise."

"Are Grandpa and Grandma coming, too?" Ryan asked hopefully.

"Yes, honey, but not until a few days later," Susannah explained. "They have several parties to attend around the holidays and you know Grandma has her big New Year's Eve party to plan. She has to finish making all of those arrangements before she can leave. But they will definitely be there before Christmas and have promised to spend as much time with you as they can."

By this time Tom had walked into the room and indicated to Ryan that he wanted to talk to Susannah before he hung up. "Okay," Ryan said, satisfied that he would see his aunt soon. "Dad wants to talk to you. Bye." He handed the phone to Tom.

"Hi, Susannah," Tom said cordially, "how are things in Philadelphia?

"Everything's fine here, but I miss him. It's just not the same around here. It's kind of boring, actually," she said with a laugh, "and quiet, too. So very, very quiet."

"Not here," Tom replied jovially. "In fact, it's quite the opposite. I had no idea an eight-year-old could generate so much chaos! And where in the world does he get all that energy?"

Susannah laughed on the other end of the line, remembering how active a boy that age was.

"I'm sure you know exactly what I'm talking about," he added.

"Yes, I do," Susannah agreed. "Yes, I do."

"I just wanted to tell you that I got your email with your itinerary. I'll turn up the heat on Friday so it'll be nice and cozy when you get here on Saturday."

"Thanks, Tom," Susannah said. "I appreciate you keeping an eye on the place for me. Do you have plans this weekend? I promised Ryan I would take him Christmas shopping for you and Annie when I got back."

"That's no problem at all," Tom assured her. "I knew you would want to spend some time with him so we left the weekend open."

"I appreciate that, Tom," Susannah said.

"The only commitment we have is to spend Christmas Eve at Annie's house. Did you talk to her about that?" he asked quickly, wanting to be sure Annie had extended the invitation to both Susannah and her parents.

"I did," Susannah assured him. "Mother and Father will be arriving the day before Christmas Eve and are looking forward to having dinner with your friends and family. They are especially looking forward to meeting your parents, Tom."

"Unfortunately, they won't be attending this year," Tom said apologetically. "They had a prior commitment they could not easily change."

"I'm sorry to hear that," Susannah said sincerely. "I'm sure they would change their plans if they could.

We'll just have to make arrangements to meet them another time."

As planned, Annie's parents arrived three days before Christmas. They had all been looking forward to this visit for months and it was finally here. Scott offered to pick them up at the airport and Annie had gratefully accepted.

Final preparations for the party had been underway since shortly after Thanksgiving, but there was still so much to do. Her mother had offered to help with the baking so they would start on that tomorrow. Tom had been great about putting up the outdoor decorations. He and Scott had hung the outdoor lights the day after Thanksgiving and he was currently in the process of decorating the hay wagon they had attached to Grandpa Ben's old tractor.

Becca's son Drew had suggested the hayride and Tom seemed delighted. He'd spent many hours tuning up the old tractor and fixing the tires on the trailer. He mapped out a route around the property and bought fresh hay from a farm up the road so the kids could have a true hayride experience. He planned to surprise them as soon as Paul and Rachel arrived with their children. Annie had no doubt the kids would love the surprise as Tom had planned a scavenger hunt along the way.

"It will be so nice to have kids here for the party," Annie told her mother as they worked together in the kitchen later that afternoon. "I know Ryan will enjoy having other kids to play with."

"Do you miss teaching?" Mary asked her daughter.

"A little," Annie admitted, "but not as much as I thought I would. I think it's because of my work at Magnolia Lane. I know they aren't kids but I truly love visiting with the residents and bringing them some small measure of joy with my flowers. They have been such a big hit, Mom."

"You've done an amazing job with the store, Annie," her mother said. "It seems like you have really found your calling."

"And then there's Ryan. I love that boy like he was my own child," she said tenderly. "I still can't believe how much my life has changed since I came here. I couldn't be happier."

"I know," her mother said lovingly, smiling warmly at her daughter. "I see it on your face and hear it in your voice. You have a wonderful circle of friends, young and old, and a terrific man in your life. I see how you are when you are with him, Annie, and I couldn't be happier for you."

"He really is a great guy, Mom," Annie said earnestly. "He is kind and has a huge heart. But most importantly he's a man of honesty and integrity. He always tries to do the right thing. That is so important to me. You know how hard it was for me to trust again after what happened with Jarrod."

"I know, honey, but that's all behind you now. You came through it stronger and more self-assured, with a clear idea of what you want out of life. And just look at what you have accomplished since then. You have a wonderful man who loves you, friends who treasure and adore you, a home where you least expected it, and a future that is literally blooming!"

Annie laughed at her mother's reference to the flower shop and hugged her tightly, spreading baking flour over them both. "You're absolutely right," Annie said confidently, "I have everything I ever wanted and more than I could have wished for. It certainly is a Merry Christmas!"

"Sir, I'd like to talk to you about my intentions with Annie," Tom said when he found himself alone with Pete Reed. He'd been trying to maneuver the situation for hours and he finally got his chance when Annie and her mother went upstairs to wrap a few last minute gifts.

"Oh?" Pete replied, turning to look at Tom expectantly.

"Yes, sir," Tom began, suddenly nervous about speaking to Annie's father. "I want you to know that I love your daughter very much and I only want what's best for her."

"And you know what's best for her, do you?" Pete asked, staring at Tom intently with his eyebrows raised, interrupting his obviously prepared speech and enjoying it just a little bit as Tom squirmed under his gaze. But Pete just didn't have the heart to let the young man suffer further. The truth was that he respected Tom for coming to him to ask for permission to marry his only daughter. So, before Tom could respond, Pete smiled at him and said, "Tom, you're a good man for coming to me first and I'm only giving you a hard time because I like you."

"Well, that's a relief." Tom laughed. "I was beginning to wonder if I was going to get through this. I don't know why I'm so nervous. I love Annie and I can't wait to ask her to marry me. I guess part of it is because it's not just me she'll be marrying. Assuming she says yes," Tom added quickly as that hint of nervousness crept back into his voice. "I mean, I'm sort of a package deal with Ryan in my life now."

Pete caught the involuntary smile that appeared on Tom's face when he mentioned Ryan. He also knew how much Annie loved kids, especially Ryan. "Well, Tom," Pete began, "I can't speak for my daughter of course, but her mom and I would be delighted to have both you and Ryan in our family. You have our blessing."

CHAPTER 37

Becca and Scott brought the kids and came over early on Christmas Eve to help Annie and Tom prepare for the festivities. Tom had the tractor and wagon securely locked away in the barn to avoid Drew and Angela getting a sneak peek at the surprise he planned for later that afternoon. Rachel and Paul would be arriving with their kids in about an hour, after picking up Eva and Lillian from Magnolia Lane. Winnie and Betty Lou would be arriving momentarily with enough pies to feed an army. With the fresh bread, rolls, and cookies Annie and her mom baked, if anyone went hungry it would not be for a lack of food.

"I'm here," Becca announced to Annie and Mary as she stepped into the kitchen, "put me to work!" The kids headed into the living room to play with Ryan and Daisy as Scott and Tom went down to the basement to bring up the extra tables and chairs they would need for dinner.

The hayride and scavenger hunt were a huge success. Tom, Paul, and Scott all got into the act by taking turns driving the tractor and riding in the wagon with the kids. Every so often they would stop and Tom would tell them a tall tale he made up just for this occasion, which ended with a list of items they needed to find. As they rounded the back of the barn and pulled up into the yard at the end of their trek, Annie and the other women in the kitchen could hear them singing and laughing with the guys. They sat on the back porch until dinnertime, comparing the treasures they had collected and recounting the stories Tom had told them. Annie thought they had enjoyed it almost as much as Tom, but she couldn't be certain. He hadn't stopped smiling since he'd started formulating his plan.

Annie had never cooked for such a large gathering, but she loved having everyone in her home. They managed to get all of the adults seated in the large dining room and the kids were happy to be by themselves at the kitchen table, Daisy lying under their feet patiently waiting for scraps. Everyone seemed to have a wonderful time. Charlotte was a bit reserved and didn't interact much with anyone except Ryan, but Frederick was quite entertaining. He was well read, well traveled, and thoroughly enjoyed regaling anyone who would listen with his stories. Tom was especially interested in Frederick's recounting of his trip to Tibet.

Paul and Scott had gotten to know each other quite well over the past several months as activities with Annie and Tom brought the families together on multiple occasions. Rachel and Susannah had developed a friendship when Susannah lived in Magnolia Creek and they enjoyed catching up during dinner.

Annie was enjoying her role as hostess. When Lillian and Winnie had approached her last summer about throwing a Christmas party, she was completely against the idea. She had never hosted an event like that and she barely knew anyone in town. *Now just look at me,* she thought to herself, *just look at the life I've created. I am sitting in my own house full of friends and family.* She could not have imagined this scene even six months ago.

"Charlotte, my dear, where did you say you were from?" Lillian asked Susannah's mother as they sat in the living room enjoying their coffee.

"Philadelphia," Charlotte replied quickly.

"Hmmm," Lillian said thoughtfully, "I have the strangest feeling that I know you from somewhere."

"I doubt it," Charlotte replied, "unless you've spent much time in Philadelphia."

"No," Lillian shook her head slowly, "I can't say that I have."

"Or perhaps you've been involved with some of the historical societies in the city?" Charlotte added helpfully. "I've been associated with quite a number of them over the years."

"No, I'm quite certain that's not it. Then again it could just be butterflies in my brain." Lillian sighed. "It's a sure sign of old age." She smiled at Charlotte sweetly then looked directly at Betty Lou.

"I wonder what that was all about?" Betty Lou said to Winnie a few moments later as they cleared away the dessert dishes.

"What was what all about?" Winnie asked, completely in the dark, having missed Lillian's look.

"She thinks she knows something," Betty Lou continued as if she had not heard her friend.

"Who thinks she knows what?" Winnie asked again as Betty Lou ignored her and walked back into the living room.

"Well, I guess she'll tell me when she thinks I need to know," Winnie said to herself and went back to scraping the dishes.

"This has been quite a day," Annie said to Tom when they finally found themselves alone shortly before midnight on Christmas Eve. Pete had convinced Mary to retire early to give Annie and Tom some time alone. He explained why only after they had said good night to their daughter and Tom, wishing them a Merry Christmas.

"You must be excited about your first Christmas with Ryan," she said to Tom, smiling at him knowingly. "Don't think I haven't noticed all of the bags and boxes you've been storing in the barn loft over the past couple of months."

"I have a lot of years to make up for," he explained. "I just hope he likes what I bought. You know, you think you really know a kid until Christmas rolls around and suddenly you worry that whatever you pick out will be wrong somehow and scar him for life."

"Stop worrying, Tom. You've already given him the best gift he could have ever hoped for," she reassured him. "You gave him his father."

"Then I guess there's only one gift left to make this a perfect Christmas," Tom said softly to Annie, motioning to Ryan behind her back.

Seeing his cue from his hiding place on the stairs, Ryan padded softly across the floor toward Annie and Tom, carrying the small jewelry box with the engagement ring his dad had picked out for Annie.

Keeping the box hidden behind his back, Ryan suddenly appeared beside his father and they knelt together, each on one knee, in front of Annie. Annie was overwhelmed with emotion as Ryan held up the ring box, told Annie he loved her, and asked her to be his mother.

Tom then took the box from Ryan and opened it to show Annie the ring. "I love you, Annie Reed. I love your easy smile and your generous heart. I love your compassion for others and your sincerity and openness with your friends and family. I love who you are with me and I love who I am with you. But most of all, Annie, I love us together, as a family," he said, pulling Ryan to his side. "Will you marry me?"

"Marry us?" Ryan chimed in with a "please, please, please" under his breath.

"Yes," Annie said to Tom, deeply moved by his proposal, "and yes, yes, yes," she said to Ryan, kissing him on the top of his head. Tom, however, she kissed squarely on the lips. He hugged them both with such force he nearly took their breath away.

"This is the best Christmas ever," she whispered to Tom as he placed his ring on her finger.